Jonathan Taylor is an author, editor, lecturer and critic. His books include the novels *Entertaining Strangers* (Salt, 2012) and *Melissa* (Salt, 2015), and the memoir *Take Me Home: Parkinson's, My Father, Myself* (Granta, 2007). He is editor of *Overheard: Stories to Read Aloud* (Salt, 2012), and co-editor of *High Spirits: A Round of Drinking Stories* (Valley Press, 2018). He directs the MA in Creative Writing at the University of Leicester. Originally from Stoke-on-Trent, he now lives in Leicestershire with his wife, the poet Maria Taylor, and their twin daughters, Miranda and Rosalind.

T0352144

JONATHAN TAYLOR

SCABLANDS

AND OTHER STORIES

SALT
**MODERN
STORIES**

SALT

CROMER

PUBLISHED BY SALT PUBLISHING 2023

2 4 6 8 10 9 7 5 3 1

First published in Great Britain in 2023 by
Salt Publishing Ltd
12 Norwich Road, Cromer, Norfolk NR27 0AX United Kingdom

www.saltpublishing.com

Salt Publishing Limited Reg. No. 5293401

A CIP catalogue record for this book is available from the British Library

ISBN 978 1 78463 294 6 (Paperback edition)
ISBN 978 1 78463 295 3 (Electronic edition)

Typeset in Granjon by Salt Publishing

Printed and bound in Great Britain by Clays Ltd, Elcograf S.p.A

For Karen Stevens

Me only cruel immortality
Consumes: I wither slowly in thine arms,
Here at the quiet limit of the world,
A white-hair'd shadow roaming like a dream
The ever-silent spaces of the East,
Far-folded mists, and gleaming halls of morn.

— ALFRED TENNYSON, 'Tithonus'

We only see what we have missed. All is in retrospect.

— KATHERINE MANSFIELD,
Letter to Sydney Schiff, 1921

He would like . . . to awaken the dead and to piece together what has been smashed. But a storm is blowing from Paradise; it has caught itself up in his wings and is so strong that the Angel can no longer close them. The storm drives him irresistibly into the future, to which his back is turned, while the rubble-heap before him grows sky-high.

— WALTER BENJAMIN,
Theses on the Philosophy of History

Contents

A Sentimental Story

REDUNDANT, DIVORCED, BENEFIT-CAPPED, Eleanor needed a job, and she needed one fast – or she'd lose her basement bedsit for good. But no job seemed right; no-one seemed to want her. She spent days wandering up and down the high street, asking in shops, hairdressers and cafés, weaving through great swarms of people. The swarms never stopped moving – and she felt as if everyone except her had someplace they had to be, someplace that wasn't here, and she wondered where it was.

She wondered too what all these people might be missing – what she could provide that they didn't already have, what job she could do in this city that wasn't already taken. For a week, two weeks, three, she had no ideas. The city didn't seem to need her, and she felt invisible, ghostly, as if the crowds might pass straight through her. So many people, yet none of them seemed to touch her, or touch one another, for that matter – everyone swirling between, around one another in fast-moving, fractalic patterns.

Then, one day, desperate, distracted, she bumped into

an abandoned newspaper kiosk, right in the eye of the commuting storm. Everything seemed to go quiet around her, as she opened the plastic door, stepped inside, and hovered there for a moment, shifting her weight from one foot to the other. It was tiny: built for one person to sell newspapers through an aperture at the front. On the floor was a box half-filled with year-old newspapers, out-of-date headlines.

On a whim, Eleanor ripped off a piece of cardboard from the lid, pulled out a lipstick from her handbag, and wrote in large capitals:

HUGS – 2 MINUTES, £2 EACH
KISSES – 2 MINUTES, £5 EACH

She propped the makeshift notice up on the tiny counter. Then she waited.

"It'll never work," someone shouted to her left.

She looked round: there, in a doorway, was a bearded guy in a faux-Burberry cap, ensconced in a sleeping bag, waving a can of max-strength lager.

"It'll never work," he repeated – but more softly this time, as though he were blessing the idea rather than predicting its failure. He grinned and raised the can in salutation, and she turned back to face the oncoming crowds.

She waited. Sleeping-bag guy watched.

She waited – and gradually, ever-so-gradually, they started to come: apologetic questions over the counter, tentative knocks, embarrassed faces coalescing from the blurred crowds, sliding coins towards her. "Please may . . ."

"I'm sorry to bother you . . ." "If you're serious, I wouldn't mind . . ." "Do you really mean . . . ?"

Yes, she did really mean it: she'd open the door, let affection-starved strangers into the tight space of the kiosk, and hold them tightly against her, or kiss them on the cheek, lips – simulating whatever kind of relationship, maternal, paternal, fraternal, erotic, they were missing or had lost.

Sleeping-bag guy looked on open-mouthed, as first a trickle and eventually – over the next few weeks – dozens, even hundreds of lonely people hesitated in front of the kiosk, then queued, knocked, and helped her scrape together enough for rent and a sandwich. It seemed the city was brimful of loneliness – it came down with the rain, puddled underfoot.

There were children who had no attention at home and only tests to look forward to at school, who saved up pocket money for her; there were travelling salespeople who missed their spouses, and needed someone to touch; there were shop assistants on their lunch breaks; there were exhausted nurses who'd watched someone die at work, who stopped off on the way home to empty flats; there were runaway sons, bereaved daughters, divorced husbands who brought her flowers – one who even proposed to her.

And, of course, even though the kiosk was in the middle of a busy street, and everything that happened inside it was visible, there were still a few – but only a few – creepy, unpleasant, or aggressive customers: the men who pressed their erections against her; the men who groped her; the drunks with bad breath; the jealous ex-wife who slapped her; the man who snogged her and then punched her in the stomach – just as her ex-husband had once done, when, for the fourth month in a row, she hadn't conceived; the teenager who ran off with the day's profits; the stag party that tried to cram into the kiosk, chanting "Get your tits out! We're having a gangbang!" – until a policewoman chased them away.

The policewoman herself was a regular customer. Before she came across Eleanor's kiosk, her only physical contact was with muggers and binge drinkers: pinning back arms, pushing people face down on the pavement. So when she discovered Eleanor, rather than asking her if she was aware that she was trespassing, that she had no right to use this property for commercial purposes – that, though long-abandoned, this property belonged to the bankrupt local newspaper – rather than doing her so-called "duty," she slipped £2 across the counter, and stepped inside for the first hug she'd had in a year. It was lovely, the two minutes over all too soon. "I'll come back," she said, wiping away tears. And she did.

"I think she likes you," shouted sleeping-bag guy, after one of the policewoman's many visits. "Good move, getting the local pigs on side."

"Shut up," Eleanor shouted back. But she was smiling, and handed him a tenner at the end of the day. He gave it back to her the next morning. "But you need it," she said. "You look thinner every day."

"So do you," he said. Then he grinned: "You can't get too thin, you know. No-one'll want to hug a fucking skeleton. See the ten quid as an investment. Like me buying shares in your company. I'll expect some bloody amazing dividends at the end of the financial year." He looked up, as if into the future: "I can see it now: a few months, and

I'll be moving out of this mansion into something even more palatial. You never know, it might even have walls."

The months went by: seven days a week, rain slanting through the aperture, ice jamming the door, heat laminating the huggers in sweat, Eleanor was always there, while sleeping-bag guy watched, incredulous. She caught viruses, mouth ulcers, even – once – nits from her customers; every night she went home to her bedsit exhausted, her arms aching, her lips sore. But she kept coming back – as if she felt she deserved these things, as if there was nowhere else she could go.

"You're amazing," sleeping-bag guy shouted at her one evening, as she was shutting up shop. "At this rate, you really are gonna get rich. I wish I'd fucking thought of the idea first – though I don't suppose anyone'd want to hug me." Eleanor blushed and looked away, didn't answer.

The next morning, he was gone. His sleeping bag was still there, as were his empty cans of max-strength lager, even his faux-Burberry cap. But he was gone.

Eleanor asked the assistant manager from the shop next door – who popped in every morning on her way to work for a cuddle – if she knew where he was, but she had no idea. Had hardly noticed him.

Eleanor asked every customer that morning if they'd seen him, but no-one knew him, no-one had given him a second thought, even though he'd been sleeping in the same doorway for months.

By the end of the day, her arms ached, her lips were bleeding from a man who'd bit her – and she was crying for the first time in months. It didn't seem right, carrying on as normal with the empty doorway to her left. She felt spectral again, while the city crowds were surging up around her kiosk, preparing to swamp her with loneliness.

More than anything, she wished she'd given the man in the doorway one freebie, one hug. She couldn't believe, now he was gone, that it had never crossed her mind. Maybe that last thing he'd said had been a hint. Maybe now it was too late.

The final customer of the day was the policewoman. "Can I come in?" she asked.

Eleanor opened the door and let her into the tiny space. This time, for a change, the policewoman hugged her, put her arms round Eleanor. Eleanor pressed her head against the policewoman's chest, cried, told her about sleeping-bag guy.

"Do you know where he is?" Eleanor asked. "Do you have any idea where he might've gone? Please, I know it sounds strange, but I felt he kind of . . . watched over me. I sort of feel like he was, I don't know, my manager, my shareholder, even . . ."

"I don't know," said the policewoman, "but I can try and find out. If you like, we could try and find out together." The policewoman hesitated, looked straight into Eleanor's eyes. "In the meantime, can I give you £5 this time? Would you mind, Ellie, if today I . . . ?"

"No," said Eleanor. "I really wouldn't."

Bee in the Bonnet

For M.

EMMA WAS LEVITATING again, a foot above the bed. It wasn't uncomfortable, just a little cold on her back, because the blankets didn't float with her. From the bunk above her own, she could hear her sister's slow, wispy breathing.

Minutes or hours went by – of her sister's breathing, of sheep she couldn't count above five-ish, of strange creaks from downstairs, of staring at patterns in the wooden slats just above her.

Finally, bored of levitation, she drifted to a sitting position, and then stood up, feeling the carpet's wool between her toes. Her sister muttered something and the upper bunk creaked.

Emma stepped away from the bed, over corpses of discarded teddies, to the door, then tiptoed onto the landing. She knew where she was going. She wanted to find her mummy, feel her warmth. She never levitated in Mummy's bed.

The door to Mummy's room swung open. She stepped inside.

It was much lighter in here, and her eyes took a moment to adjust. The windows were open and a breeze blew moonlight into the room.

"Mummy?" whispered Emma.

But her mummy wasn't there. The bed was empty, the covers pulled back.

She'd never seen the bed empty at night before. She wanted to cry.

She looked through the open windows to the moon, which seemed no more than a step away from them.

Perhaps, she thought sleepily, Mummy had flown away.

She wandered round the bed to the window.

In front of her were stars and planets. They looked huge, and she wondered if, once upon a time, they'd all joined up, like a magic carpet or rainbow.

She wanted to touch them, so she hoisted herself onto the window frame. She could feel splinters jabbing into her feet.

She took one foot off the frame, reaching out for the moon.

She breathed in, leant forwards.

The door in the room behind banged open. She may or may not have heard her sister scream: "*Emma!*" – but couldn't be sure, because she'd already gone.

There was a whooshy noise like wind, a dizziness, a headache, as all the colours in the sky smeared together. A second or month passed.

Now she was in a park. It was afternoon – a sunshiny-daffodilly day. In front of her was the façade of a ruined castle – roofless, windowless, with red and orange walls, jagged crenellations, stone staircases leading nowhere.

She ran barefoot across the lawn. People were dotted about, but no-one seemed to notice she was still in her Andy Pandy nightdress, which flared out behind her.

Panting, she reached the spot where she knew her mummy and sister would be. She sank down on the towel they'd spread out for a picnic. It was a banquet of triangular sandwiches, hard-boiled eggs, sausage rolls, coffee in a flask.

She stuffed a triangle into her mouth. She thought Mummy might tell her off for leaving the bedroom, coming to find them here. But her mummy didn't – and instead seemed to stare straight through her. She felt invisible, a ghost at the picnic. And, in turn, she couldn't quite see her mummy's or sister's faces: the sun was too bright, shooting right through them.

Dazzled, Emma looked away, scanning a tumbledown wall behind their shoulders, about a hundred yards away. An exposed stone staircase with no handrail jutted out of the wall. Towards the top she could see someone – who was it? – oh, how funny: it was herself, in miniature, skipping down the steps. As if, at that moment, she'd split into two selves, two ghosts – one watching, one skipping.

There was no handrail.

"I love you," the self on the lawn murmured, overcome with happiness – but she wasn't sure which light-silhouette she was saying it to: her mummy, her sister, or her other self, tottering distantly on the stone stairs.

"It never bloody well happened," says her sister. She prises the toast out of the toaster with a knife, puts it on a plate, and butters it, ferociously.

"It was *so* vivid, Suze," says Emma from the kitchen table. "I can remember everything. I can even taste the cheese sandwiches."

Her sister plonks the plate in front of Emma, turns to make the tea. "Dreams can be vivid, Em, especially when you're a kid. But it's all rubbish. Let's forget about it."

Emma nibbles a corner of the toast. She wonders if it's wrong that what her sister thinks is a "dream" is a favourite childhood memory: should something (supposedly) made up trump reality?

"I hadn't thought about it for – I don't know – thirty years or something," says Emma. "Or perhaps it's thirty-one years. No, it must be thirty." She frowns, mouthing the numbers to herself, shakes her head. "But anyway, it all came back when we were in the crematorium. It's my earliest memory. I could have only been three or four. Tiny."

"It's not a memory," says Susan.

"Don't ruin it for me, Suze." Emma taps the side of her own head. "You think it's because of this." Her bottom lip wobbles.

"Oh come on, Em. You're not three now. It was years ago." Susan sighs. "Like everything."

Emma lowers her gaze. "But . . ."

"You do go on. It's like Mum used to say: you get bees in your bonnet. Buzz buzz buzz. Haven't we got enough on our plates? Let's just focus on sorting out the house – it's going to be hard enough without you banging on about flying and sausage rolls."

Emma nibbles another ashy crust, then puts the toast down. She doesn't feel hungry, hasn't felt hungry since the funeral – wonders if she's really felt hungry since a long-ago picnic at a ruined castle.

"Perhaps it's a real place."

"It's not," says her sister. "I don't want to talk about it any more." She pulls herself to her feet, leaves the room.

"What if it turns out it's real? What then?" Emma asks to thin air.

Thin air and her sister ignore her. The latter calls from the hallway: "Best get started. Let's try and rescue some stuff before the vultures arrive. Then I've got to get home to feed Chris and the twins. Then work. Then, then, then."

"What if . . . ?" dreams Emma.

Later, Emma finds a box in a corner of the attic, trapped in webs as fine as her mother's hair. It's full of old Super-8 cartridges. Her sister wants to bin it: "The films, they won't have survived. And any that have'll burn up if you try and watch them – like the last time Mum used the projector." But Emma holds the box to her chest, won't let it go. Huffing and puffing, she struggles with it downstairs, deposits it on a kitchen chair, and fetches the Yellow Pages. Eventually, she finds someone who can transfer cine-camera film to VHS.

It's towards the end of the second cassette that she sees the ruins. The hairs on the back of her neck prickle up.

There it all is from her dream-memory: the castle, the picnic, the hard-boiled eggs – everything weirdly translucent, pierced with white light. It's silent: the camera, which must have been held by her mum, pans unsteadily over the picnic, to a tiny Susan, cheeks full of food; then it moves to the ruins – which are more greeny-grey than orangey-red on the film – and then, with a jerk, it flicks up some stone stairs to zoom in on Emma, who's skipping down them, waving at the camera, sticking out her tongue. She's moving quickly, two steps at a time, unfazed by the lack of handrail.

Then, for some reason, there's a blur, and the scene ends with a close-up of sandwiches and feet, the world tilted at a vertiginous ninety degrees – and a blue flame flickers across the TV screen, consuming everything. The next scene that emerges from the flame is their old backyard, months, maybe a year later. Emma presses stop, rewind.

"I saw it. Honest, Suze. It's on the film. Here." Emma thrusts the video cassette into her sister's hands. Her sister glances down at it, turns it over, turns up her nose.

"Oh," she says, her jaw set.

"I saw it," says Emma. "It's the same castle. It's real. It's a *real* castle somewhere, and we had a picnic."

"So what?" asks her sister. She tries to give the video back.

Emma shakes her head. "No no no. You have to see it. You always say I'm imagining things. Getting bees in my bonnet."

"I don't want to see it. Look, Chris'll be back soon. I need to make tea. So if you'll . . ."

"Please, Suze. Then you'll see everything was real."

"It wasn't *all* real. You didn't fly or teleport or whatever from Mum's bedroom."

Emma isn't listening. "I wonder where the castle is. You might know when you watch it. Or we can try and find out. Then we can go there, you and me. Like, together." Susan doesn't answer. "I know Mum won't be there so it won't be the same. But we can still have a picnic and . . ."

"I'm too busy. I've got so much to catch up on after the last few weeks. And I can't abandon Chris and the twins just like that." She snaps her fingers. "Chris is already pissed off with me as it is."

"Please, Suze."

"No," says Susan, decisively. "I don't want it. I don't want to see it." She shoves the cassette into Emma's hands, and swivels round to slice the vegetables. She wipes her eyes with the back of her wrist – the onions, thinks Emma.

Emma hovers, shifting her weight from one foot to the other, waiting for an opportunity to hand the video back. But Susan doesn't turn round again, and hums tunelessly to herself, to stop Emma saying anything else.

Emma spends next day in the library, surrounded by books about castles. She narrows her search down to the Midlands – her mum never drove too far on day-trips.

All day, she pores over pictures of castles, leaning in close – as if trying to break through the pages into the places themselves. She copies down their names into a note-pad, so she remembers which candidates she's eliminated:

Warwick Castle: no, too grand.
Stafford Castle: wrong shape. Not big enough.
Nottingham Castle: not country-side-ish enough.
Shrewsbury Castle: close, but too un-ruined.

Kenilworth Castle: close, very close. A bit too ruined.
Ludlow Castle: oh . . .

She holds back tears from dripping onto the page. She thinks she's found it. She wants to go there – perhaps fly there – now, this moment. But she can't fly any more, can't drive, has never been on a train. And anyway, she's already late for Susan, who she's meant to be meeting at 5, back at Mum's old house.

The house is finally empty, ready for the sale. The sisters wander through it like memories or dreams, figments of the house's imagination. Emma feels like she's floating – can't hear her own footfalls.

They've dusted, hoovered, mopped, scrubbed. Still everything looks dirty, tired, the ruins of a family home. There are imprints of furniture on carpets, wardrobe shadows on walls, spidery cracks in corners. Curtainless windows stare inwards at the sisters.

In the hallway, Susan turns to face Emma, waves a duster at her: "For the last time, Em, I can't drive you to Ludlow."

"Why not?" asks Emma. "It's such a tiny thing to ask. You and me."

"It's always one tiny thing – then another tiny thing. Bees in bonnets. Buzz buzz."

"It's the only bee I've got."

"At the moment. Anyway, I can't drive you there."

"Why not?"

"Because I don't have a car any more," says Susan. She turns, starts climbing the stairs one last time.

Emma frowns at her, tugs her sleeve. "Why? What's wrong with it?"

"Gosh," says Susan. "You're *so* like Mum. Endless bloody questions." She sighs and pivots round to face her sister again, holding onto the banister as if she might fall – or fly away. "He . . . Chris took the car."

"I don't under . . ."

"He's left, Em." She realises she's going to have to spell it out: "*Left me.*"

Emma's eyes widen. "Oh," she says. "You mean like divorce or something?"

Susan nods and sinks down on the step. "He gets the car, I get the twins and . . . so I can't drive you to Ludlow, Em. It's a struggle just getting to work."

"Oh," Emma says, sitting down on the step below her sister.

"There wasn't any shouting," says Susan. "He just told me, all matter-of-fact, he couldn't cope with things any more – you know, twins, funerals and . . . other stuff." Susan doesn't tell Emma that the other stuff includes a semi-dependent sister. And Emma doesn't guess what she's left out.

Instead, Emma mouths: "Oh," once more and, for the first time in years, loosely takes hold of her sister's fingers. She flinches a bit at the physical contact, but doesn't let go, doesn't yell.

They're frozen there for a few minutes – Emma not knowing how to break the contact, Susan not wanting to.

Susan wipes her eyes with the duster in her other hand, blinks through the dust, and says: "Come on."

"Come on what?" asks Emma. They stand up, still holding fingers.

"Come on," repeats her sister. "I can't take you to Ludlow, but – " She leads Emma up the stairs, onto the dark landing, and into their mum's old room. There's no bed, no wardrobe. Emma feels her lips moving: "Mummy?" but no sound comes out.

The windows, which reach almost floor to ceiling, are wide open, and a breeze from who knows where – perhaps a faraway castle – is touching their faces.

"Come on," says Susan again, and slips off her shoes. Emma does the same. They hoist themselves up and stand on the low window frames. There are no splinters underfoot this time round, just lukewarm PVC.

Susan knows what to do, because she saw her sister do it once before, thirty years ago – though she always pretended she remembered nothing of that night, was instructed *never ever ever* to mention it, or any subsequent flying incidents, *in case . . . In case* of what? – she isn't really sure, now she thinks back, what threat or danger the words *in case* actually implied. Repressed for so long, her own memory of it all is sketchy: there are the moments of clarity – waking up in the middle of the night, wandering into her mum's empty room, seeing her sleep-walking little sister balanced on the sill, screaming and grabbing her, just before she tumbled – and there are the moments of darkness, when a blue flame consumes everything – like the long-suppressed afternoon, weeks or months later, when a little sister, who had a bee in her bonnet about flying, ran off during a picnic, got lost in a castle, and dived or tumbled, head-first, from one of its walls.

It's almost dark outside. There's no moon, and the stars and planets are few and far between, hazy, dusty – as if they've been moving away from one another, shrinking, since the sisters' childhood.

The sisters perch on the sill, feet arched over the frames, hands holding the sides, fingers touching.

Stepping out, they both know, is the only way back *there* – the only way back to sunshine and castle and picnic and sausage rolls, before . . .

Susan sighs, sits down, lets her legs dangle over the edge of the past. Tells Emma to do the same.

Staring Girl

A T ELEVEN, THE girl who would grow up to be a famous horror writer fell in love for the first and only time. She fell in love with another girl in her class, a girl who never spoke to anyone but herself – a girl who stared silently, intently at the other kids, as if crucifying them one by one with her gaze. If this made everyone else in the class wriggle uncomfortably, if this made everyone else push her around during break-time, asking her what the hell she was staring at, why the hell she was such a freak, it made the girl who would grow up to be a famous horror writer fall deeply and irrevocably in love with her.

It happened one morning, when the sunlight was penetrating the dingy classroom in shafts, impaling one pupil after another. Staring Girl seemed almost transparent when the girl who would become a famous horror writer glanced up from her exercise book, and realised she'd finally been picked out by that stare. Staring Girl had never chosen her before, and she'd always wondered why. For a few moments, she returned the stare, and, instead of feeling outraged, of wanting to punch Staring Girl's lights out, she smiled back and almost sobbed

– as though the stare had unleashed something deep inside.

At the end of the lesson, as the girl who would become a famous horror writer was packing up her things, she felt something brush against her elbow, and turned to find Staring Girl next to her. Staring Girl was holding out a sheet of paper. The other girl took it and looked down: it was a drawing of her face, beautifully, carefully outlined and shaded. She was going to say: "Thank you," but Staring Girl had already wandered off absent-mindedly, no doubt to be shoved around in the playground, spat at.

◊

After that morning, Staring Girl started sketching all the other pupils in the class. The teacher didn't seem to care what Staring Girl did, never once singling her out, or telling her off for incessant doodling. The only person in the class who took any notice of her drawing was the girl who would grow up to be a famous horror writer. She kept looking over, to see if Staring Girl was staring at her, drawing her. But she wasn't, not any longer.

Instead, every lesson, Staring Girl drew at least one or two of the other pupils. At the end, she would quietly pad up to them, offering them the drawings. Generally, the kids tore up the portraits in her face and threw them in the bin.

Over the weeks, as the summer holidays approached, the portraits began to change slightly – imperceptibly at first, as if they were drifting bit by bit towards carica- ture. Lines were sometimes more wobbly, cheeks more flabby, noses distorted, eyes bloodshot and shadowed, hair receding, deep-set wrinkles scarring childhood faces. Facial hair sprouted prematurely, teeth went black and fell out, blood vessels burst, lines spread like spiders' webs. Eventually, disease, advanced old age, even, in some cases, the greens, blues and purples of decomposition settled over childhood faces, like a spectral palimpsest, as though both layers could co-exist in a single sketch.

The other children in the class were horrified, destroying their portraits with the fury of miniature Dorian Grays. Some cried and told the teacher. Some punched Staring Girl out in the open. One knocked her over, and stuffed the portrait into her mouth, holding her mouth shut till she swallowed. No-one stopped what was happening, no-one intervened.

The girl who grew up to be a famous horror writer didn't join in with the other kids, but didn't intervene on Staring Girl's behalf either. She watched from a distance, ashamed of herself and aching, aching to be drawn again.

◊

Finally, one morning in mid-July, she was. At the end of a Maths lesson, Staring Girl tiptoed up to her, and handed her a picture which she should have found disturbing, shocking: it was her own face, but creased, ancient, withered, petrified with decades of loss and loneliness.

Rather than feeling disgusted, she looked up from the sketch and kissed Staring Girl. Only on the cheek – Staring Girl was already turning to leave, and the girl who would grow up to be a famous horror writer only caught her there. Still, it was the kiss of her life.

Staring Girl hesitated, touched where she'd been kissed, and then left for the playground – where she was kicked and spat at and called a freak, a weirdo, a fucking retard until she cried. Some of the girls held her down, whilst a big boy pushed a stick into both eyes to stop the horrid staring once and for all.

◊

Staring Girl had black eyes for a week, infections for longer – and, from then on, never once looked up from her desk, never drew any more pictures of the other pupils. None of them missed the attention, except the girl who loved her. She'd wander over to Staring Girl's empty desk during break time, to see what she'd been doing.

It turned out Staring Girl was still sketching – but now it was just her own face, over and over again: lines hazy, shading paler each time. Unlike the earlier portraits, she never aged on these mirror-pictures, always stayed eleven. The girl who would grow up to be a famous horror writer took one of them, and slipped it into her rucksack, hoping Staring Girl wouldn't notice, wouldn't say anything.

Staring Girl didn't, because next day she stopped coming to school. No-one mentioned her. The other pupils were relieved she was gone. The teacher didn't explain her absence, and, after a few days, moved her desk and chair out of the way.

When the holidays came, the girl who would grow up to be a famous horror writer cycled round to Staring Girl's house and stared at it from a distance. Stared and stared, until her eyes ached. The family was still there, silhouetted behind the curtains; but there was no sign of *her*.

The girl who would become a famous horror writer cycled round every day that summer, watching the front door, willing it to open; but Staring Girl never came out of it again.

◊

Decades later, exhausted from writing, loss and loneliness, the old woman who was once the girl who would grow up to become a famous horror writer has lit a huge bonfire in front of her house. She's burning all her books, all her letters and photographs, furniture, even some of her children's toys. Words, chairs, faces, animals, dollies, dozens of staring eyes flare up, blacken, melt in the fire. She wants rid of everything now she is going blind, now she is dying. There's something satisfying about watching your whole life go up in blurry smoke, she thinks.

The last things she casts onto the flames are three sheets of paper, which are now blurry, clouded by cataracts: two childish drawings of herself – one young, the other as she is now – and a sketch of a girl she once knew, a girl who never changed, who never aged, a girl eternally eleven.

Not a Horror Story

THE NEW RESIDENT was disappointed in the house. No blood dripped from the walls. The doors didn't shut by themselves. There were no bangs, murmurings and cries during the night. That bothered her more than anything: the quiet, the stillness. When her husband was away and the bed was empty, there wasn't even any breathing.

A house like this, where such horrors had taken place – where, according to the local paper, a neglected child had been cut up and left to die – shouldn't be quiet. She knew that from *The Shining*: the house should *remember* – it should remember why they'd got it so cheap, in an otherwise-desirable North London cul-de-sac. The horrors that had happened within these walls – though they weren't extreme enough for the house to have been bulldozed – should have left traces, ghosts, scratching in the walls, strange flowers flourishing in the garden. Instead, it was neat, carpeted, magnolia.

She decided to make up for the house's lack in this respect by painting the front room scarlet. Ignoring her husband's half-hearted criticisms, she purposely left drips drying in the paint, to look like blood.

Next, she drilled a large hole in the ceiling above the landing, all the way up to the attic, in order to create the kind of cold spot she had seen in any number of horror movies.

At night, when her husband was away, she'd leave the radio on downstairs – quiet, detuned – so disembodied voices, fuzz, pops and screeches reached her in bed.

She bought a doll that intermittently gurgled and cried, and buried it underneath one of the loose floor-boards in the front room. As the batteries in the doll gradually wore out, the noises deepened to baritone, distorted into growls. Her husband didn't notice, didn't seem to hear it, when back home from his business trips to Bangkok, or wherever it was he went.

And none of it – not the paint, the hole in the ceiling, the radio, the buried doll – had any more effect on her than on her husband. She didn't feel the cold in the cold spot; the hairs on the back of her neck stubbornly refused to stand on end whenever she heard radio or doll; her body refused to tremble in the dark; and her dreams remained undisturbed, suburban, bloodless, magnolia.

She felt nothing.

So finally, one night when her husband was away again, she wandered downstairs into the kitchen, took out one of the steak knives, and made cuts in her arms and legs, not unlike those she had seen in the newspaper photos of the dead child.

At least, she thought, the cuts hurt.

Zoë K.

Excerpts from the Private Journal of Dr Christopher Sollertinsky

Wednesday 20 April, 1994.
Third day of my secondment. Still haven't unpacked; hotel room full of boxes. Couldn't face it. Instead, went straight to hospital.

First outpatient appointment was talented (and *very* striking) young woman, Zoë K. Resembled the ex when I first met her – many years ago. Unlike the ex, Zoë is fascinating, a unique case. Since a bicycle accident and subsequent coma, her mother told me Zoë has trouble recognising places. Specifically, she keeps saying, "I want to go home," even when at home, in her own living room. When challenged about her delusion, Zoë declares: "I know it looks like home, and my piano sounds a bit like the one at home, but they're obviously fakes. I want my *real* home with my *real* piano." Have referred patient for CT and MRI scans. Suspect some peculiar form of delusional misidentification syndrome – probably reduplicative paramnesia (RP).

Zoë K.

Friday 13 May, 1994.

Met with Zoë K. again today to discuss results. Scans confirmed right central hemisphere and frontal lobe damage, in the form of ischaemic lesion, probably a result of earlier trauma. Damage is concordant with suspicions of RP. Consulted with colleague, who confirmed my tentative diagnosis, though remarked on the case's anomalies: the patient is young (twenty-two years old), charming, intelligent and well-spoken in other ways, and exhibits little or no paraphasia, psychomotor issues, or cognitive deficiencies as a result of her accident, twelve months ago. Indeed, apparently she still plays the piano up to a near-virtuosic standard – and recalls pieces which she played before the coma with ease. So at present her delusional inability to recognise home manifests itself as a peculiarly isolated symptom.

There are, of course, no proven pharmacological treatments for RP. I decided to trial her on the anti-depressant citalopram, and the anti-psychotic haloperidol. Will reassess this intriguing case in two months. Looking forward to it – wish it could be sooner.

Thursday 9 June, 1994.

Had an emergency referral from Zoë K.'s GP. Citalopram and/or haloperidol having unexpected side effects, exacerbating her condition. Tried to explain to Zoë and her mother that the side effects are temporary, the treatment needs more time. Both clearly distressed. Mother told me Zoë won't sit still at home for more than a few seconds and is always getting up to leave – to find, as she puts it, her "real home." Even packs a suitcase sometimes.

Mother doesn't know whether she should be locking Zoë up, or letting her out. Zoë distressed too because she finds it difficult to sit down at the piano to play: "It's not *my* piano. It only looks like and sounds like my piano. And when I try and . . . play, I can't find the end . . . I can't find the end of pieces." I asked her what she meant, but she couldn't fully explain because of her overwrought state. No doubt due to this nervous excitement, for the first time she exhibited symptoms of aphasia in her speech.

As an amateur musician myself, am fascinated by her unusual symptoms. So have agreed – in a purely private capacity, of course – to visit her at home, in order to understand her condition more fully. There may be research funding in this case somewhere – and, you never know, another secondment away from poisonous ex-wife.

Tuesday 21 June, 1994.
Visited Zoë K.'s house. As soon as I was ushered into living room by the mother, Zoë jumped out of her chair and burst into tears: "I'm so glad you're here, doctor. I need you to take me to my *real* home. No-one else understands me except you." I was touched by her faith in me. I quietened her down, and reassured her that I'd see what I could do.

In the meantime, I asked if she would play the piano. At first she refused, claiming it wasn't *her* piano, and it sounded ever-so-slightly out of tune. I insisted, though, and she sat on the stool, lifted the fallboard, and started playing – without a score, or any further prompting – the opening movement of Schubert's late B-flat Sonata. At first, I was astounded by the fluency, the beauty of her playing. Normally reticent and dependent on her mother – it seems to me, from my limited observations hitherto – in music she gained an assertiveness and emotional expressiveness I'd never have anticipated. Her treble playing was lyrical, songful, and I've never heard those spectres at the feast – the dark trills in the bass which puncture the songfulness throughout the first movement – sound more haunting. In those trills, it seemed as if she were somehow recalling the darkness of her coma; and in listening to her playing, I felt I myself were sharing her memories, her experience.

Or at least, that was the case through the exposition and development sections: as she approached the recapitulation of the main theme, the music seemed to float away, repeat itself, disintegrate into echoes, until all that was left were the bass trills – and then suddenly she broke off and burst into tears. She grabbed my hand and wouldn't let go. I asked her what was wrong, and she sobbed: "I just can't find it," over and over again. I asked her what she couldn't find, and she said: "Home. I can't find the way home. It never sounds quite right."

It suddenly struck me what she meant: it would seem that Zoë has not only lost home in terms of physical place, but also in music. Here we have a bizarre, synaesthetic form of RP involving not merely impairment to the visual processing systems, but also to the auditory cortex. This is a spatial *and* musical reduplicative paramnesia, and could represent a landmark case in conceptions of neuropsychology. I myself feel disorientated by this, as if a new neuroscientific vista has opened up to me – so much so that I tripped over on the doorstep as I left the house and twisted my ankle.

Tuesday 28 June, 1994.

Visited Zoë K. again yesterday. Listened to her playing sonata movements by Schubert, Beethoven, Mozart: in all cases, the music became improvisatory, polytonal and eventually disintegrated in the latter part of the development sections, as she struggled to find "the way home," as she put it – that is, back to the home or tonic key. There is nothing but *becoming* in her playing, only the journey out, never the return. Her music is homeless, a permanent refugee, if you like.

After three pieces, I suggested she try something more modern, without so firm a sense of home key. She reached under her piano stool and pulled out a score of *Nuages Gris* – a late, experimental work by Liszt – which she proceeded to sight read. In it, I heard the dark trills of Schubert's B-flat Sonata join up, shutting out the light. Here, there is no true recapitulation, no return home, no reassuring sense of cadence – and, as such, the piece embodies what one might be tempted to term a kind of *musical* paramnesia. For these reasons, Zoë managed to play it to the end. She was crying with happiness: "I reached the end," she said, "I reached the end of a piece for the first time since the accident." Then she gave me a hug and wouldn't let go. I didn't mind, because I too was happy for her.

I suggested from now on she concentrate on playing late Liszt, as well as twentieth-century atonal composers. She has all the makings of a modernist virtuoso, I think. Her playing is earworm-like: back at the hotel, I had dreams filled with dark trills all night – as though trills, paramnesia, brain lesions were somehow contagious. Finally woke up in the dark and couldn't find the light switch.

Zoë K.

Friday 1 July, 1994.
Visited Zoë again today. Unofficially, of course. Just wanted to learn more about her case. And hear her play. She seems to enjoy my visits as much as I do. She played Schoenberg's *Six Little Piano Pieces* for me. Her touch had the sharpness of a scalpel, the precision of a dissection. Felt as if my own brain were on the operating table. Afterwards, was so dizzied by it all, I drove round and round in circles, kept taking wrong turns. Something's happening to me I don't quite understand.

Monday 4 July, 1994.
Okay, I confess – to you and you alone, diary – I can't keep away from Zoë and her playing. I know it's wrong in *conventional* terms, but what can I do – what could anyone do – when faced with this unique case, this kind of playing? And when did conventional behaviour ever produce a scientific breakthrough?

This evening, Zoë played Webern's *Variations for Piano*. Made me feel like everything was crumbling to dust, everything was disintegrating, that nothing connected to anything else any longer. Afterwards, struggled to find the front door to leave, as if my brain didn't want to leave – and then kept dropping my car keys. Couldn't find the door handle of the car. Finally pulled myself together and drove back to hotel.

Tuesday 5 July, 1994.
However tempting it is, I won't go. Honestly, I won't go. Shouldn't go. Mustn't go.

Friday 8 July, 1994.
Went to visit Zoë. Her mother was out. She played Boulez's Second Piano Sonata. Felt speechless, paralysed, comatose. She took my hand and led me upstairs to what she said wasn't really her bedroom. We made love on the bed she said wasn't hers. Or at least, we tried to for half an hour. Neither of us could reach orgasm. Mother came back early and almost caught us.

Beginning to think we'd *both* make a good case study or research project.

Saturday 9 July, 1994.
No, I won't go. Won't go. Won't go.

Sunday 10 July, 1994.
I tried to go but couldn't find her house. Drove round and round in circles. Eventually gave up and came back to hotel room. Would have called her, but worried her mother might pick up the phone.

Monday 11 July, 1994.
Dreamt all night of grey clouds swirling, swirling, never stopping. Phoned in sick. Was sick. Stayed in hotel room all day. Desperate to see Zoë, but daren't go out in case I can't find my way back.

Tuesday 12 July, 1994.
Someone must have moved me while I was asleep. I seem to be in the wrong hotel room.

Zoë K.

Wednesday 13 July, 1994.
I want to see Zoë. I want to go home. I want to see Zoë. I
want to go home. I want . . .

"But what happens after?"

. . . Ginny asked.

"What do you mean, *after*?" I asked. "It's Beethoven's Fifth, for goodness sake, Ginny. There is no *after*. That's it. The end. *Kaput*, as the Germans would say."

"Don't quote Germans at me, darling. I've had enough of them for a lifetime. They never stop, musically or . . ."

"I'm not quoting. I'm just saying. That's it: perfect cadence to final C major chord, blazing triumph, the end. There's no *after* to Beethoven's Fifth."

"There's the clapping we're doing now."

"That's not part of the music."

"And then there's us leaving here, my wheeling you out to the park, us . . ."

"I know, but it's not like a sequel. Music doesn't have sequels or postscripts. Well, except for some excruciating claptrap by that Wagner chap. The music ends, and that's it – back to life. Life and music, they're two separate spheres. You do talk nonsense sometimes, Ginny."

"Don't be all cross, all *supercilious* with me. It's not my fault. It's the music's fault. It's the music that makes me feel like this, you know. Even when it's playing, it seems like it's never going to end. Like Beethoven can't quite find the end, keeps looking round corners, opening doors. So the end, when it does come, feels glued on, fake, like it could actually go on forever. The tunes are still going on in my head, round and round. Do you see what I mean?"

"Not really, Ginny. An end like that, it seems pretty final to me."

"Nothing's ever *really* final," she said.

"What do you mean?" I snapped.

"Well, look at . . . I don't know . . . the war, for example."

"I don't want to," I said. "We've come out *not* to look at it. It's over now, and no-one wants to hear us talking about it. Everyone's looking at us, Ginny."

"But it's not over," she said more loudly, stamping her foot, as if she didn't care who was looking at us. "Every Christmas, when it was meant to be over, it wasn't. Every bit of leave you had felt it was over, but it wasn't. And even now all the fighting's stopped, it's not over. It'll never be over. There's no Armistice in our heads, you know. The war, it's like a Beethoven tune that keeps going round and round up there." She tapped the side of her head.

"You're talking nonsense, Ginny. Getting yourself worked up. We'll get you home. Perhaps tonight's been too much for you."

"Don't patronise me, darling. You don't understand. You don't see that *every* night has been too much for me. And now you're back, it's still too much. I waited for you all that time, we were engaged all that time, and now you're back, it's no different. Or it is different, but it isn't. Oh, I don't know."

She cried a bit, then grabbed her coat, pushed past a whole row of people trying to clap, and was gone.

I wasn't sure whether she was gone for good.

◊

Along the line, Captain Salter is playing a gramophone record of Beethoven's Fifth back at them – over the mud, across the craters, through the barbed wire. He's deliberately playing it at the wrong speed, slowly-slowly-thump-thump-thump-crackle-crackle, mocking them. When they used to play it to us before, it was like artillery fire. Now, at this rpm, it sounds weary, raggedy, defeated. Like them, the poor bastards. Beethoven's triplets are dragging their injured legs through excrement.

Me, I'm sitting – actually *sitting* – cross-legged on the top, in the putrefying mud, blowing smoke rings, whistling along to the stretched-out notes, thinking that soon, so soon, the music will be over, maybe even soldiering will be over. No more tin hat, no more box respirator, I'll be demobbed and back with Ginny. She's waited a damned long time, bless her.

Before that, some of the lads have been given the job of shovelling out bits and pieces of our friends in the mud, dumping them into sandbags. I'll give them a hand in a moment, rolling back the wire, uprooting the posts, searching craters – and, you never know, once done, sharing a smoke with the very people who were trying to kill us a couple of days (which seems like a hundred years) ago.

None of us believed it when the official message filtered down. No-one believed the rumours of talks, church bells, flags and dancing in London, Paris. No-one believed the rumours from elsewhere of white flags, collapsing lines, Mons retaken, Boche pushed back to the frontiers. Nothing like that had happened here. Here, at 11 a.m. on the 11th, it was quiet, like it used to be before the blasted planes swooped over. Further up, you could still hear muffled shelling, machine guns, the howitzer on the hill, all carrying on as if nothing had happened, as if they wanted to use up the ammunition while they could.

But now it really does seem to have stopped. *Kaput.* And the chaps in front of me are snipping through the wire. One of them seems to have got his boot caught. I'll go and help him in a minute.

But at this precise moment, sitting here in the sun, blowing smoke rings across no-man's-land, hearing Beethoven stretched on the rack to my right, I wonder if this is the happiest I will ever be.

Of course, it's all too easy to forget, when one is mad with happiness like this, and the bloody farcical horror of it all seems over and done with, that there are still mines hidden out there, waiting to blow off one's legs.

◊

I could hardly chase after Ginny, so I stayed where I was while the clapping finished, people picked up their programmes and coats, started to file out.

I stayed put until everyone had gone, and someone was brushing between the rows in the gallery above, humming Beethoven to himself. He glanced down at the stalls and saw me sitting there: "Do you need any help, mate? They don't make these places any good for people like you."

I shook my head and wheeled myself out – and from there all the way to Holland Park.

I wheeled myself to a corner of the park where Ginny and I sometimes . . . met. I sat facing the wall. I wanted the wall to block everything out.

But it didn't block everything out. I could still hear Ginny's voice, on and on in my head.

I sat there and thought about her words, my wheels sinking into mud. It was quiet, dark. There might be a storm. Distantly, as if from across a vast no-man's-land, there was thunder. I glanced up at the sky, and the gaps between the clouds looked like rolls of barbed wire. I stared instead at the wall, and in the bricks I saw rows of covered corpses, the lined-up dead. I looked down, and the dark spaces where my shins used to be were the shape of shells.

I shut my eyes.

Behind my eyelids, I saw-remembered the first evening Ginny was allowed to visit me in St. B————'s. She didn't say anything, didn't even cry. She bent down and lightly kissed the spaces, the empty trouser legs. And believe it or not, I felt those kisses – as if her lips were telling me that the legs weren't really gone. That nothing and no-one is ever really gone.

I turned away from the wall, headed back home.

"You keep it"

"NO, YOU FOUND it, so you get to keep it."

"You have it."

"No, honestly, you keep it. You might need it."

For a moment, she sounded almost offended: "Why do you think *I* might need it? I don't. Honestly, I don't. I don't want it. I want to give it to you. *Please* take it."

They'd found it lying under the park bench, half covered by sludgy brown leaves. It must have fallen out of someone's wallet or pocket. Nobody was around. There was no-one to give it to, no-one to ask if it belonged to them – well, except a tramp huddled up and snoring on the bandstand.

She scrunched up the note – as if the Queen's head were so much rubbish – and shoved it into her son's pocket.

"You have it."

"Muuuuum . . ." He elongated the word, in a descending musical scale.

"Don't worry, Jase, you can, like, pay me back a thousand percent interest when you've graduated. When you're cutting up all those private patients on Harley Street or wherever."

"Muuuuum . . ."

"Please, Jase. *Please*. Just have it. All the other mums and dads come here and take their kids out to Sainsbury's or bloody Waitrose. At least I can give you this." She changed the subject, before he could object, or say anything else. "Look, I tell you what, let's go and grab a proper drink before I have to leave."

"Why do you *have* to leave, Mum? Why do you have to go so early? There are later trains back."

"There's something I've gotta do."

"Oh." He thought for a second and frowned. "It's not anything to do with that bloody Kensington bloke, is it? Bastard. *Bloody bastard*."

"Please, Jase. Please. Don't talk about Mr Kensington like that. We owe him a lot. We owe him, and he's been . . . good to us. Or, at least, he's not been awful to us, which he could've been. When, y'know, he had every right to be."

Together, in silence, they wandered out of the park and back into town.

They wandered past boarded-up shops, cut-price card shops, temporary pop-up shops, loan shops, betting shops, chip shops, shops with the wrong names over their fronts, market-stalls selling second-hand pants, empty market-stalls selling nothing. They wandered past a half-derelict church, deserted warehouses and a brothel, nicknamed by locals A Pound of Flesh, which had a 'For Sale' sign pasted over its windows – as though even sex had gone bankrupt in this town. For one painful moment, she wondered if this really was the land of milk and honey – of opportunity, education, hope – that she had dreamed about for her son.

The pain passed as it always did; and the two of them

carried on wandering, across a stagnant canal, and then past a terrace where an old man was hunched over an organ, his front door ajar, polluting the street with Bach. Finally, they stopped at The Bitter End, a pub near the station, and stepped inside its grubby twilight.

He hadn't taken his mother to his regular pub, because he didn't want her to hear the bar people say his name. He didn't want her to know that they knew him – knew him, in fact, better than his course-mates or uni lecturers.

At the bar, he handed over his credit card, not the scrumpled-up note in his pocket, to a barman in a string vest. Then he carried two double shots to a table in the corner, where his mother was already sitting.

"I miss you, Mum, when you're not here," he said quietly.

"You shouldn't, Jase."

"But I do."

"Don't be silly, darling. Don't think about me. Enjoy yourself."

"Are you enjoying *yourself*, Mum? Or, at least, are you taking care of yourself?"

"Yeah. Of course. And you?"

"Yeah. Course."

Neither looked at the other while they said these things. The table, the bar-mats seemed far more interesting. Jase was shredding the mats one by one.

There was a pause, then she said: "Are you, like, doing well at all the studying and lessons and stuff, Jase?"

"Mum, don't go on."

"I knew I didn't have to ask. I knew you would be. Honestly, Jase, I'm bloody proud of you, y'know."

"Muuuuum . . ."

"No-one in our crappy family's been to uni before, you know that. As if they would've been – bunch of bloody numpties, 'specially on your dad's side. None of them – including your dad – could hardly spell better than the dog. Let alone be a doctor, like you. A doctor, like you, *my Jase*."

"Muuuuum . . . I'm not a doctor yet. Nowhere near."

"You will be, Jase. I know it." Without thinking, she glanced at a watch on her wrist that was no longer there, and then up at the clock over the bar. "God, the time – I've got to go for the train now, Jase. I'll miss it otherwise. You stay and finish. Have another. No need to get up."

He took the note they'd found earlier out of his pocket and smoothed it flat. He placed it on the table between them. "Mum, please take it. *Please.* You probably –" he hesitated, and then decided he might as well carry on, say what he was going to say: "You probably need it more than I do."

"Don't be stupid. Whatever gave you, like, that idea? I'm fine. Honest, I'm fine, darling. You're the one who's racking up massive amounts of debt, with all those bloody loans you have to get. You're the starving student, Jase, not me. I'm fine. Honest. I swear."

"But Mum, you found it. Take it. It could pay for your train fare. Well, some of it."

The note seemed to hover, levitate, on the table between them, buoyed up by tiny breezes, shallow breaths, a fan heater behind the bar, love. Mother and son stared down at it, transfixed – as if, for these few moments, their lives were centred on this note – as if the note were the only positive charge in their world, while everything round it was negative, minus, in the red – as if everything else were boarded-up shops, tramps, string vests, debt, parting.

Neither of them took the note.

"I don't want it," she said finally, pushing it back towards her son. She could have added: "It wouldn't be more than a drop in the ocean, anyway" – but didn't.

Instead, she stood up, put on her coat, kissed her son on the forehead, squeezed his shoulder, and left him . . .

. . . left him to *not* keep the money, which he handed instead to the tramp on the way back to his flat – a flat where he would *not* spend the next few months studying, where he would *not not* spend all his time being home-sick, avoiding other students, skiving lectures, missing his exams, crouching behind the door if anyone knocked – and nipping out, away from campus, when they gave up – because he felt more at home drinking in The Bitter End, or one his regular dives – or swapping booze and fags with bandstand-tramps – or wandering round decaying shops – or listening to Bach fugues played by a dying man to an empty street . . .

. . . while his mother travelled back home by train to an empty flat – to *not* pay the debts for her son's living expenses which she owed to Mr Kensington – or, at least, to *not* pay them in money, but in the only way she had left – and then *not* to cry, or *not* to *not* cry, or *not* to *not-not* cry, or . . . well, what did it matter? It was all the same now, on her own, without her son.

Till Life

10.02 a.m.
Here I am again, like usual, sitting behind the till, waiting for a customer to come into the shop. *Lahlahlahlahlah.*

10.44 a.m.
Here I am still, sitting behind the till, waiting. Tuesdays are slow days, and today is Tuesday. At least I've got some digestives under the counter.

10.47 a.m.
Still here at the till. Mrs Parker says I should always be ready, even if there are big gaps. Mrs Parker's the manager of Hurt Heads. She's also my mum, but I'm not allowed to call her that in the shop.

She says it's the *ultimate irony* me working for Hurt Heads, after what happened. She also says I don't know what irony is so not to worry.

The only thing I'm worried about now is that it's cold in here. So I'm putting on my coat. Hidden in one of the pockets is a tea-cosy – well, it's a hat, really, that belonged to someone else once. But it looks like a tea-cosy, all knitted and patterny. I keep it in case the someone else comes back in the shop. If Mum found it, she'd go ape, yelling stuff about *fair-weather friends* and *dangerous driving* and *Prosecco*. I don't think that would be irony.

11.04 a.m.
I'm humming a tune: *Lahlahlahlahlah*. I can't remember what the tune is. Perhaps when Mum gets back I'll ask her – I mean, Mrs Parker.

Mum says music is *good for mindfulness*. She's got *The Beginner's Book of Mindfulness* at home. She says that since the accident we all have to *concentrate on the moment, not dwell on the past, or worry about the future*.

11. 06 a.m.
So here I am, concentrating on this moment: sitting-waiting-sitting-waiting-humming-waiting-not-eating-digestives. This moment's a bit boring, to be honest. Hope it'll be gone soon.

11.18 a.m.
I'll have a digestive at 11.30 if no-one's around. I know that's thinking about the future, but it's only a few-minutes-away-future, so maybe it doesn't count.

11.27 a.m.
Three minutes till digestive-future.
Lahlahlahlahlahlahlah.
Oh, a customer is coming into the shop. Boo. It's kind of like a train announcement: *Unfortunately, we're sorry*

to report that your digestive is delayed. We apologise for any inconvenience caused.

11.33 a.m.
The customer, who's wearing a tie with helicopters on it, is buying *Greatest Hits of Black Lace* and a small china dog which nods when you touch its head.

I do all the things I'm meant to: I take *Greatest Hits of Black Lace* and small china dog off him, look at the price stickers, tap the numbers into the till, press MISC, then SUB-TOTAL. I have to hold SUB-TOTAL down for it to work. It's an old till, as old as my mum, and not like the high-tech ones they have in Asda.

While I'm holding SUB-TOTAL down, I like to imagine everything and everyone stops for a second – you know, like musical statues. Even the people outside the window freeze. Sometimes, when I'm on my own, I press it down to see what happens, if anything moves. It's like the world is holding its breath in – *concentrating on the moment*, as Mum says.

As soon as I let go of SUB-TOTAL, I have to do lots of other stuff – counting change and offering a bag and saying thank you, and Mr Helicopter Tie says "Thank you" back and nods, over and over again, like a small china dog.

11.34 a.m.
At last: digestive time.

1.35 p.m.
I haven't had any lunch, only six digestives, so I'm all tummy-and-headachy. Headaches make my thoughts get

all jumbled. Mum says whenever I feel like this, I should focus on what I'm doing now, and the feeling'll go away. But the problem is that I'm not doing anything now.

Instead I'm remembering this thing from a few weeks or months ago, and the funny thing is that it feels in my head like it's happening now: a lady is coming into the shop. She's got what looks like a tea-cosy on her head, with knitted flowers on it.

Tea-cosy lady is picking up a saucer – it's one of those willow-pattern ones – and looking at the price underneath. She brings it over to the till. She's staring at me and coughing. So I'm coughing too, cos it might make her feel more comfortable. Then suddenly she's asking: *Do you know who I am?*

I'm looking at her face under the tea-cosy, and as if by accident I'm saying to her: *I don't remember your name but I think you're one of the fair-weather friends my mum talks about. You were driving the car and didn't visit me in hospital.*

Tea-cosy lady's eyes are all watery and trembly like bubbles. I'm wondering if you pricked them with a pin, would they burst. I haven't got a pin so instead I ask her: *Would you like to gift-aid the saucer?*

She shakes her head. Then she grabs my hand and it's a bit too tight and she's crying like somebody has actually popped her eyes and saying lots of sorries without taking a breath. She pulls out a bunch of chrysanthemums from one of her bags and holds them out to me, crying big tears all over them. They are beautiful and rainbowy and crinkly. The flowers, not the tears.

Later, though, my mum comes back and asks who they're from. And next morning, when tea-cosy lady is in the shop again, Mum appears as if from nowhere. She's shouting things at tea-cosy lady which don't sound very mindful or irony-ish. She knocks tea-cosy lady's tea-cosy off, and pushes her out the door. Tea-cosy lady doesn't say anything. She just looks at me with those bubbly eyes through the window, and runs off, leaving her tea-cosy behind. My mum forgets about it, and I pick it up and put it in my pocket when she's out back. It's my one and only secret.

2.04 p.m.
No customers. Nothing to do. *Lahlahlahlahlahlah-lahlahlahlahlah.*

2.44 p.m.
I've run out of digestives. Boo.

3.56 p.m.
I've been here for a year and a half now. I don't mean I've been sitting behind this till for a year and a half – although it kind of feels like that. I mean I've been working in Hurt Heads shop for that long. At least, I think it's that long. It's hard to remember when most days are the same. My mum says *it's good experience – gets you back out there.* I'm not sure what I'm supposed to be experiencing *out there*, or here, well, apart from sitting and waiting for my mum, I mean Mrs Parker, to come back to cash up. Waiting for going-home-time.

I know it's bad of me, but the funny thing is I don't want it to be going-home-time *or* sitting-in-the-shop-time either. Both are Mum-I-mean-Mrs-Parker-times. I think, before the accident, I used to have some non-Mum-times. I wish I could remember them now.

I wonder if the tune that keeps going through my head – you know, the one that goes *Lahlahlahlahlahlahlah* – comes from those before-times.

3.59 p.m.
I'm staring out of the window, and suddenly I'm looking at her: tea-cosy lady – well, tea-cosy-lady-without-the-tea-cosy.

She's near the shop window. I want her to look in. I want her to stop. I don't care about *fair-weather friends* or *Prosecco* or *dangerous driving* or *irony*. I want to hold her hand again and give her her tea-cosy back.

Oh no, I think she's walking past.

I want her to stop.

I am pressing the SUB-TOTAL button on the till.

I am holding it down.

Outside the Circle

RACHEL HOVERS JUST outside the circle. "My brother said . . . I mean, *says* it's the *real shit*." She tries to sound convincing, authoritative: "And he knows his stuff." She's conscious of a wobble in her voice, but hopes the other girls won't notice.

There's a pause. Everyone looks at Aly, whose eyes are narrowed on Rachel, sussing things out.

"Okay," says Aly, holding out her hand. "Everyone knows your bro knows his stuff. *His* name's cool round here" – unlike, presumably, Rachel's – "so yeah, hand it over and we'll try it."

Rachel glances around. "Here? In the . . . park?"

Aly stares at Rachel like she's stupid. "Yeah. Here. In the park. In the open."

"Okay," says Rachel, her voice wobbling even more. She injects confidence into it, trying to sound like Aly: "You're on." She takes the sachet out of her blazer pocket, and places it into Aly's outstretched hand. Aly's fingers close over it.

Aly looks around, and behind her, where there's a hedge and an orange sign: NO ALCOHOL. FINE

£150. BY ORDER OF LEICESTERSHIRE COUNTY COUNCIL. "We're in the perfect place," says Aly to the group, motioning for them to sit down. "We'll sit here, under this sign. It's not like we're drinking alcohol. Besides which, if we do get done, my old man'll pay for us all. It's his fucking job."

Four girls sit on the cool grass. Aly looks up at Rachel, who's still standing. "Sit down, for fuck's sake," Aly says. "You're annoying me up there. Blocking out my sun. Suze, Beck: make room for Rach."

Rachel tries not to beam, just nods, and takes her place between Suze and Beck.

Aly's already hunched over, working on the spliff. She's taken out a Maths textbook from her bag, and has carefully spread out what she needs on top of it: two Rizlas, filter, lighter, tobacco, and a bit of what Rachel has given her. Rachel watches her work – they all do, quiet now.

Aly carefully places the roach at one end of the Rizlas, then spreads out the tobacco. Next, she takes the stuff Rachel brought, and almost sprinkles it – with a delicacy Rachel wouldn't have thought possible of her – over the tobacco. She starts rolling. Finally, she licks the spliff closed, twists the end, and holds it up, proudly. Behind her, Rachel hears a passerby with a dog mutter something, and carry on walking.

"Behold, like, *the master's work*," declares Aly, grandly. Suze and Beck giggle. Kelly, on the opposite side of the circle to Rachel, claps. Rachel smiles half-heartedly, thinking how quickly, effortlessly, almost balletically her brother used to roll a spliff in comparison. She suppresses the thought – which is in danger of ruining her mood – and joins in with Kelly's clapping. "Now," says Aly, sparking up, "we shall sample our new friend's offering."

Rachel's smile is genuine now. She looks down at the grass in front, trying not to go red at the word "friend," trying not to betray herself.

Aly has noticed, though: "Mate, you haven't even fucking tried it yet, and you're already looking stoned. We're going to have to work on you – I can see that. Not cool. Get a grip."

Rachel nods. Aly takes a big drag on the spliff. She holds it for a few seconds, then coolly exhales. She doesn't cough – just clears her throat a bit.

Suddenly, she's shouting: "What you fucking staring at, mong? Fuck off." For a horrible moment, Rachel thinks she's the one being shouted at. But swivelling round, she sees a red-faced boy on a bicycle cycling away. "Twat!" Aly shouts after him. She takes another drag of the spliff, and passes it to Kelly on her left.

Kelly does her best not to cough: "Wow," she says, after a couple of drags: "Just wow. Good one, Rach . . . and yeah, of course, Aly."

Next up is Suze. She does cough, and Aly grins at her: "Mong," she says. Suze scowls, but two or three drags smooth out the scowl, and she lies back on the grass giggling. She holds up the spliff for Rachel to take.

Rachel takes it. It's gone out, so she reaches for Aly's lighter with her free hand. One of Aly's Doc Martens crushes her hand on the ground. Rachel yelps.

"That's mine," says Aly. "Use your own. I'm not that stoned yet."

"Okay," says Rachel. She prises her hand from under

Aly's boot and reaches into her rucksack. Somewhere at the bottom is one of her brother's lighters. Aly stares at her while she rummages through exercise books, papers, old makeup, hairbands, pens.

"Fucking get on with it," says Aly.

Rachel goes red again, thinks she'll never find the lighter – until, finally, she touches something metallic, a tiny, grooved wheel. She fishes it out and – on second try – manages to relight the spliff. She takes two drags, doesn't cough and passes it on.

"Smoked like a fucking pro," says Aly, arching an eyebrow. "Impressive for a mong."

Rachel squints at Aly – the sun is almost directly above her – and then lowers her gaze to the grass again. "I've had a bit of practice," she says. She doesn't add: probably more than any of you.

Beck, meanwhile, has been struck down by a hacking cough. She's taken in too much at once. She's coughing so loudly she's attracting attention from a few people across the park. Aly kicks out at her. "Shut the fuck up, you stupid fuck." Even Aly's bravado has its limits, Rachel realises with a clarity lent to her by the spliff: even Aly, openly smoking weed in a public place, doesn't want attention from the wrong people. "Shut the fuck up," Aly hisses again. Beck gets up, leaves the circle, and runs to throw up in the bushes.

"What a mong," says Aly to Rachel, smirking, "two puffs and she's out."

When Beck – pale and out of breath – re-emerges from the bushes, Aly grins at her: "God, you stink, Beck. Got vom on your skirt. Fucking disgrace – can't even handle a bit of this shit. You need to learn from pros like me and Rach here." Rachel smiles at the grass again – until Beck, rejoining the circle, accidentally kicks her knee while sitting back down. Rachel flinches, but doesn't say anything, just rubs the place where the tights are now torn.

Aly has been smoking all the while, ignoring Kelly's jealous stare, which says quite clearly: *pass it on, pass it on, pass it on* – although she doesn't dare say it out loud. The spliff is almost finished. Aly holds up the remains in front of her, admiringly. "Well done, Rach. This was good. Very good." She puts on a posh voice, like a connoisseur appraising a cake or wine on TV: "Yes, your brother's reputation is well-deserved. An excellent vintage, my dear. Your bro certainly knows what he's talking about when it comes to *the real shit*. You must be very proud. And you must introduce us one day, Rach, dear. I hear on the grapevine he also possesses a mighty fine c . . ."

All of a sudden, Aly stops, and looks up, out of the circle. Rachel follows her gaze, swivels round. Everyone does.

Standing behind Suze, hands in his armpits, wearing a Ushanka hat, dirty brown fleece and combats, is a young guy – unshaven, unwashed, smelling of dead leaves.

"What the fuck you looking at?" asks Aly, back to her usual voice.

"Is that a spliff?" asks the guy.

"Who wants to know?" asks Aly.

"Me," says the guy. "I'm . . . call me Jules."

"I'm not going to call you anything, creep."

"I just wondered . . ."

"What did you wonder?" asks Aly. "Can't you see we're busy?"

"I just wondered if . . ."

"What?"

"I wondered . . ."

"You just wondered if you could have a drag? Is that what you're tryna say?"

The guy nods. He's sweating, staring down at the smouldering end of the spliff as if mesmerised, in a trance.

Rachel thinks Aly is going to tell him to fuck off. In fact, everyone thinks she is going to tell him to fuck off – even the guy himself, who has shaken himself out of his trance, and is starting to turn away.

But she doesn't tell him to fuck off. Instead, she says slowly: "Okay. There's not much left. But okay, yeah, go on then, *Jules*. You can have a puff."

She stands up. The whole circle of girls stands up with her, as though she's a queen, or mistress of the house.

Aly steps across the circle, holding out the spliff, with the roach pointing towards the guy's mouth. He licks his lips. Suze sidesteps out of the way.

Aly is now face to face with the guy. They're almost the same height. If anything, she's slightly taller than him, and broader in the shoulders.

She places the roach between his lips. He takes a deep drag – it's still lit – holds it in, closes his eyes. For a moment, everything is still.

"Like it?" asks Aly, taking the spliff out of his lips, and letting it fall. He exhales to one side. She licks her lips. The two of them are close enough to kiss.

"Lovely," says the guy. "Best thing I've had for days. Fucking bliss."

"Good," says Aly. "Perhaps you'll like this too."

And she head-butts him, hard, on the bridge of his nose.

There's a crack. He yelps, falls backwards, clutching his face with both hands. "What the . . . ?"

"Fucking *mong*," she says, half-laughing, half-dazed herself. "You stink. I'll need to shower in bleach when I get home." She kicks one of his knees with her Doc Martens. "At least I've got a shower." She rubs her forehead, staggers a bit. Kelly, Suze and Beck run to hold her up. "Twat, you hurt my head."

Suze giggles, still stoned. Kelly spits at the guy. Blood is seeping between his fingers, down his arms, onto the ground. He's bent double, crying, trying to back away. "What the . . . ?"

"Fucking mong," says Aly again. "Fuck off back to nowhere." She turns away from him, still reeling. "Rach, make yourself useful, for fuck's sake. Get my phone out my bag. Ring my dad. Tell him to come and get me. Tell him some fucking homeless mong hit me."

Rachel steps over to Aly's bag and starts fishing round for her mobile. "Yeah, Rach," says Aly loudly, "tell my dad to come to the park in his *Land Rover Discovery*." She turns to face the retreating guy one more time, pulling herself up straight: "Get that, mong? – my dad's *Land Rover Discovery*. He'll fucking run you over on the way home. *Home* – hear that? – we've got one, y'know: six fuck-off bedrooms and a hot tub." She tries to laugh, flips him the bird: "Now you can fucking do one, *Jules*."

The guy, still clutching his broken nose, whimpering,

turns and stumbles away. Across the park, Rachel sees him veer off, as one of the wardens – who, like a number of people, has been watching from a distance – tries to catch him. The guy scrambles over a wall and is gone. The warden gives up and starts striding towards the girls.

"Y'know what to say, don't you?" asks Aly. All the girls in the circle nod, except for Rachel, who's still hunting for Aly's mobile in her bag. Aly glowers at her. "You know what to say, don't you, *Rachel*?" Head bowed, Rachel nods – as if she's being told off by a teacher.

She goes back to searching for Aly's mobile, finds it, and starts scrolling down contacts for 'Dad' or 'Home.' Aly steps over, and snatches the phone off her. "Yeah, well, we'll leave my dad out of it, after all. He's probably, like, busy at work or some shit. Doesn't want to be bothered with bollocks like this."

She snaps the mobile shut. They all pick up their bags, and traipse back to college. Lunch break is over.

◊

At the end of the day, Rachel runs all the way home. She bursts into the house, and takes the stairs in twos, up to her brother's room. No-one's there, of course, to ask her what the hell she's doing, to tell her to get the fuck out. No-one's been there now for two weeks.

She pulls out the drawers of his desk, lifts up the mattress, stands on a chair to feel the top of the wardrobe, and eventually finds what she's looking for. She shoves it in her blazer pocket, and runs back down the stairs, and out of the house, slamming the door behind her.

Then she runs towards town – until, out of breath, she has to slow to a brisk walk. She walks through the park, and round and round the shops, not going into any. She walks round the pedestrianised market square, up and down side streets, alleyways, across carparks. She doubles back, peering into disused units in the shopping centre. She even circles the public toilets.

Eventually, she finds him, his legs in a sleeping bag, in the doorway of what was once a bookshop.

"Hello, Jules," she says.

The guy shrinks from her, wide eyed. "Go away," he almost squeaks, "please."

She squats down, so she's on his level. "No, I won't."

From here, she can see his face is a mess: there's dried blood on his stubble and under his nostrils, and a blue and greenish bruise spread out, like a butterfly, round his nose. The nose itself is swollen, and doesn't look straight. He sees her looking at it, and his hand jerks up to cover his face.

"Get away from me," he says.

"No," she says. "I want you to have this." She fishes into her blazer pocket, and hands him one of her brother's sachets. "It's his last one."

The guy looks down at it, and then at her. "Whose?"

"My brother's."

"Won't he miss it? I don't want another loony coming after me."

"No, he won't miss it."

"Why not?"

"Because he's . . . he's gone."

"Where? Where's he gone?" The guy seems stuck in a cycle of questions that he can't stop asking – stupidly, automatically – about someone he doesn't know from Adam.

"I don't know. He left us a couple of weeks ago. Just walked out. Didn't even leave a note or nothing. My mum was doing his head in, I think. And I . . . And now, he's probably – well, he might be outside, you know, like you." She sits down next to the guy, and looks at the ground. "I miss him, y'know." She's crying. The guy doesn't know what to say or do. In the end, it's Rachel who takes his filthy hand and holds it for a minute.

She sniffs, breathes in, lets the sobs subside: "I wanted to say I'm sorry. I can't say it to him, so I'm saying it to you instead. I'm sorry."

Still in pain, still furious, still dazed from earlier, the guy finds himself saying: "It wasn't you. It was that other girl." He looks down at his hand in hers, puzzled why *he's* feeling sorry for *her*, and not the other way round. "You do realise," he's on the verge of saying, "that I'm the one who a dog pissed on this morning. I'm the one who's only eaten a cold cheeseburger in three days. I'm the one who got fucking head-butted." But he doesn't say these things – and squeezes her hand instead.

"It was me," she says.

"It wasn't – it was your mate."

"No, I mean it was me who made *him* go. It was me who told him to fuck off and die the night before . . . the night before he actually did fuck off. Mum was out on the piss, and he called me upstairs and said he wanted to hang out with a bong, and I said I had to do my homework – and he was dead angry and said I was a sad loser who didn't know how to chill, didn't have no friends. He said I was like everyone else round here. He said he was sick of it, sick of Mum, me, everyone and everything. He said everyone could go and fuck themselves. He shoved me out of his bedroom. So I told him if he felt like that he might as well fuck off too – fuck off and die."

She cries a bit more, then takes her hand away from Jules's, wipes her nose on her sleeve and stands up. "Anyway, have it," she says, nodding at the sachet. "A present to say sorry." She hesitates, shifting her weight from one leg to the other. "And perhaps," she says, "you won't mind if I say hello to you if I see you around."

"I won't mind," he says, honestly.

She takes a deep breath, turns away from him.

And there is Aly, right in front, staring wide-eyed at them both.

For a moment – a moment which replays the same stillness from earlier, just before Aly head-butted Jules – Rachel thinks Aly is going to head-butt her too. But she doesn't flinch, doesn't back away. Part of her thinks she deserves it.

Aly doesn't head-butt her. Her mouth opens and shuts a couple of times, and she mumbles something – something like: "I thought . . . I thought . . ." A strange expression, like a bruise, like another ghostly self, momentarily seems to overlay her face – and Rachel wonders if she too is lonely.

But then a burly man in a suit, who's standing a few yards behind, yells at her: something about getting her arse in gear, something about his being late for the shift, something about his daughter being a stupid bitch for wasting his time, hanging out with losers.

The ghost passes from Aly's face as quickly as it came, and her expression hardens. She looks Rachel up and down, turns up the side of her nose, swivels on her heels and strides away.

Rachel knows Aly will never talk to her again. She also knows she doesn't care.

Fleeced

LISA'S SITTING ON the park bench, facing the pond, holding a can of Diet Coke and a doughnut from Greggs. At the opposite end of the bench is an older man who she doesn't know. The only thing they have in common is their gingerish hair, though Lisa's is scraped back into a ponytail, so looks darker.

She's wearing old jeans and a baggy top she borrowed from her mum. It says: *I'M OUTTA YOUR LEAGUE* in white letters across the chest. The man is wearing a thick fleece, its collars pointing upwards, despite the late-spring sunshine.

"Why're you wearing that?" asks Lisa, without looking around. Her forehead is creased, and she's staring at algae on the pond as if it's a puzzle to solve, a maths equation at college.

"Because I'm cold," says the man in the fleece. He isn't staring at anything. He's just concentrating on breathing: in-out-in-out.

"Yeah, you probably are," says Lisa. She lifts the doughnut to her mouth and takes a big bite. As she chews, some of the jam oozes onto her lower lip. With her right index finger, she swipes it off, then holds it up to Fleece Man.

"Wanna lick that?" she asks.

"No. I mean, *not here*," he says.

"Embarrassed, are you?"

"Course I am," he says. "Anyone could see us."

"Ashamed of me, are you?"

"No. I mean, yes. Not of you – but of, well, *us*."

Lisa stares at him, as if he were algae. "*Us*? Mate, it's just you and me, separate, like. This ain't no *us* thing, y'know."

"Okay, okay," he says, under his breath. "Don't be so *loud*."

"Don't you 'okay-okay' me," she says. "I can be as FUCKING LOUD as I FUCKING want." A few ducks on the pond fly off. "I'm not doing nothing wrong. I'm just sitting on a bench, like, eating my FUCKING DOUGHNUT."

"Why are you being so . . . unfriendly? So impolite?" he asks, frowning at the pond, reminding himself that he's the older person, the one in charge. "I'm the customer, after all."

"This isn't John fucking Lewis, y'know," she hisses at him. "Take it or leave it. I'm not gonna pretend to be anything I'm not. You want some older slag who pretends to like you, all lovey-dovey-girlfriend-experience-shit, you fuck off elsewhere. There's plenty of them lot out there."

Lisa brushes the sugar off her jeans and starts to get up. He reaches over, touches her elbow. She glares down at his hand. He pulls away. "No, no, it's okay. It's fine. You're . . . perfect."

She sits back down, almost smiles for the first time.

"Well, that's not true anyway. I'm a shit. But I can help you blow your nuts, if that's what you want."

He nods. He's all hunched over now, cowed. *Good*, she thinks. *They're easier to deal with like that*. She takes a swig of Coke.

"Where we going to go, then?" he asks, quietly.

She spits the Coke out. "Y'what? For fuck's sake, mate, you should know that, not me. It's your outcall."

She glances at him. He looks like he's about to cry. She can't be doing with that – hates that kind of thing. "Haven't you done this before? Don't you get what it says on the website? You're meant to arrange a place to do it, not me. God, it's not as if we can go to mine. My mum'd kill me." She pauses. "Or she would if she weren't shit-faced."

Fleece Man doesn't say anything. He's obviously mulling things over.

"Look," she says. "I could give you a quick toss-off round the back of the caff, if we're careful. Only charge you half."

"It's all right," says the man. "My wife's out. We can go to mine. Just for a bit."

"That's more like it," she says. "Now we're getting some-where. How far away is it?"

"About ten minutes from here."

Lisa stands up, and so does he, more slowly. She chucks the Coke can into a bush. "Just remember I'm charging you for the extra time. Sitting-on-bench time. Walking time."

He doesn't hear this, and instead mumbles something she doesn't catch.

"Y'what?"

"What I said is – would you mind walking behind me a few steps? So people don't think we're together."

She grabs his hand, and presses it to her chest: "Oh, *darling*," she declaims in a high-pitched voice, "*darling*, how can you ask something like that of me? How can you disown me, after all we've been through?"

He pulls his hand away: "*Shhh . . .*"

"Oh, stop being such a wuss," she says. "There's no-one round apart from the fucking ducks. D'you think they're bugged or summit?"

"But the neighbours . . ."

"Mate, whatever. If you want me to walk behind you, pretend I don't know you – which I don't – then, yeah, that's fine. Long as I get paid. Lead the way, *darling*."

He's about to turn away and start walking. But then she clears her throat, and her eyes narrow on him: "*Ahem*, like."

"What?" he asks. "What's wrong? Don't you want to come with me now?"

"Yeah. But I think you've forgotten summit."

"What?"

"I want payment – least some payment – up front. It's, like, *standard practice*. Read the website."

He sighs and reaches inside his fleece. He brings out a fat leather wallet and takes out two twenty-pound notes. She watches carefully, peering inside the wallet, almost on tiptoes: there are a lot more notes in there.

He glances round, hands her the two twenties. She snatches them and shoves them deep into one of her jeans pockets. She nods: "Okay, let's hit the road."

He moves off, at quite a pace. He has long legs and is much taller than her.

He strides round the pond, past the war memorial and diagonally across the picnic area. She strolls after him, knowing he'll have to slow down at some point unless he wants to lose her.

They pass boys playing football, some pensioners doing Tai Chi, a couple snogging, and a group of girls, sitting in a circle, blatantly smoking weed. She can smell it a mile off. She recognises the girls from college, but looks dead ahead, hoping they haven't seen her. One of them she used to quite like, from afar. The two of them had swapped hellos and numbers once, but never called or texted each other. As for the others, she knows what they think of her – if they think of her at all. She knows they wouldn't speak to a *skank* like her, let alone ask her to join them, share their spliff.

So she might as well carry on, following Fleece Man.

She follows him out of the park, past the library, across a couple of terraced streets, down a deserted jitty called – she almost laughs when she sees the sign – True Lovers' Walk. Halfway along the jitty, he turns – the one and only time he does so during the whole walk – to check she's still following. She scowls at him, sticks out her tongue, flips him the bird. He turns away and carries on walking. "Remember all this walking time is on the meter," she calls to his back. "I'm knackered already, and we haven't done nothing yet."

Fleece Man doesn't respond. "Fuck's sake," she huffs, to herself this time.

As they carry on walking – past a playground, onto the college road – she finds herself humming something, a dismembered tune which keeps going round and round her head. She gets this kind of thing sometimes, a stupid tune which won't go away, trapped up there – like a fly or wasp, banging against the sides, trying to get out. For a while, she wonders what it is, hearing and humming it without recognising it. Then she remembers: it's bloody 'Teddy Bears' Picnic' – in the fragmented, off-key, slightly-manic version that the ice-cream van used to play, when she and her mother lived at their old flat.

At six o'clock their mummies and daddies . . .

"Fuck's sake," she hisses to the tune: "Shurrup." She can feel a headache coming on.

They're walking past the college now – the college she should be at today, but isn't. She keeps her head down, speeds up a bit, though no-one seems to notice her anyway. No-one ever seems to notice her. Sometimes, she feels invisible.

They cross the dual carriageway and take a left onto the main road out of town – and then a right and right again, into a little close she didn't know existed.

By the time she's at the top of the close, he's disappeared into one of the houses. He's left the front door open for her to follow. She does so, and kicks it shut behind her.

He's in front of her, in the hallway, hanging his fleece on the end of the banister, slipping off his shoes. He wanders into the living room.

"Are you gonna say something – y'know, like 'Welcome to my humble abode' – or you gonna give me the silent treatment like forever?" she asks after him. "No manners, some people." She kicks her trainers off, wipes her nose

on the sleeve of his fleece, and follows him into the front
room. He's closing the curtains as she enters.

"Is this when you turn out to be a psycho and cut me
up into little pieces?" she asks.

"No," he says.

They both sit on the sofa at opposite ends. The sofa's
smaller than the bench in the park, though, so they're closer
now. Sitting at an angle, Lisa lets her knee touch his. He
doesn't seem to notice. He's hunched over, staring at the
carpet.

"You must be fucking loaded," she says, looking round
at the TV, the furniture, the mantelpiece, "to have all this
shit."

"It's just a normal house," he says. He repeats himself,
his own echo: "It's just a normal house" – and it sounds
like he's going to cry.

"Whatevs."

"It's true. It's a normal house, with normal stuff and
a normal couple, who don't have sex because the wife's
always at work while the husband's on his own, most after-
noons, most evenings, most . . ."

"Oh, shurrup." Lisa moves her knee away from his.
This trick's turning out a right pain in the arse, she thinks:
a bastard of a headache, and a first-timer who doesn't
understand the deal. If there's one thing she can't stand
it's punters – and anyone else for that matter – crying.
She has to deal with enough of that from her mum.
"Fuck's sake," she snaps at him. "Let's get this straight. I
don't wanna hear any of that 'My wife doesn't understand
me' bollocks. Do I look like I care? I'm not gonna feel
sorry for you for forty quid an hour. I'm not your fucking

counsellor, and this ain't no GFE. Don't you get it? – this is a 'purely financial arrangement,' like it says on the website. I couldn't care less if you died, mate, long as I get paid."

She breathes in and out, calms herself down. "Okay, okay, bit harsh. But let's get on with it, for fuck's sake. Other hoes wouldn't be so patient, y'know."

"I'm sorry," he says to the carpet. "I do get it. I do understand."

"Forget about it." There's a pause. She sits up, composes herself, moves her ponytail over one shoulder. Then she looks at him from under her lashes, speaks more gently, rests her hand on his thigh. "Okay, then. What d'you wanna do?"

He doesn't respond. His eyes widen slightly – but other-wise, nothing.

Her tone is soft now – or as soft as she can make it: "If it's, like, something *different*, kinky-like, I don't mind. Just tell me what it is. You're paying for it."

He still doesn't respond, and she starts wriggling, starts getting agitated again. She can't stand the silence. She talks over it, tries to fill it, before 'Teddy Bears' Picnic' comes back: "Look, mate. You can't shock me. All I can say to you is no, fuck off, or yes, okay, we'll try it. I've heard it all before. I know what men are like. I mean, fuck, my own dad's a dirty bastard. You should've seen the porn he'd got on his old laptop before we sold it. And he's always, like, fucking off for weeks at a time with smack-heads and prossies. Then he comes crawling home to us on his hands and knees, wanting me and my mum to say, 'Yeah, welcome back' – wanting us to like him. As if."

You better be in disguise . . .

Her head's ringing. She stops herself, feels like she's said too much – feels like she always says too much, can't keep her mouth shut. That's what they used to say at school. They didn't understand she wasn't deliberately talking over the teacher – rather, she was talking over her own head, the noise going on in there.

She breathes in, smooths out her tone once more: "Y'know, if you want, I can suck my thumb and call *you* daddy, if that's the kind of shit you're into."

He stands up. The movement's so sudden, she flinches.

He doesn't notice, and instead offers her something to drink: "We've got Bacardi, gin, whisky, lager – whatever you want."

"You offering booze to minors, like?"

"Pardon?"

"I'm joshing you, mate. Can I have a tea?"

He frowns: "Tea?"

"Yeah, tea. Even low-lifes like me like tea, y'know." She thinks of her mother at home – probably on the bed now, sweating vodka. "It's the only thing I drink. Skimmed milk, one sugar."

Fleece Man turns, steps over to what is presumably the kitchen door, and disappears inside. Lisa can hear him clattering about the kitchen, filling the kettle, opening and closing cupboards.

She stands up and wanders round the living room, checking things out. There's a crystal vase with plastic flowers in it, on a small table next to the window. She picks it up and examines it carefully – like one of those old gits, she thinks, on *Antiques Roadshow*. It's pretty and rainbowy, but she's stupidly come without big pockets to hide anything in. She swears at herself: fucking idiot, honest by mistake. She puts the vase back down and steps over to the mantelpiece. There, she runs her fingers over various knick-knacks, vases, dolls, until she lights on a photo frame. She picks it up, and stares at the photo inside.

She hears him behind her, coming back into the living room. "This the wife, then?" she asks. "Don't look like a bitch."

"That was sixteen years ago."

"And who's the little kid next to her? Never said you had a daughter."

"I don't. We don't. She died."

Lisa puts the picture down quickly, as if it's infected with something. She rubs her hands on her top and turns to look at him.

"Sixteen years ago," he says.

"Soz," she says, automatically. Then: "Fuck, that means she'd have been almost the same age as . . ." She trails off.

He's standing, frozen, a couple of yards in front of her, holding a mug of tea. He's staring at her – for the first time since meeting, he doesn't look away – and she's staring back at him.

Watch them, catch them unawares . . .

Sometimes, she's overcome by a strange feeling she might stare at something with such intensity, it might move, even explode. Sometimes, she feels terrified by the power of her own gaze, her own thoughts – as if her headaches might kill. Now, face to face with Fleece Man, she feels, for a moment, that her gaze might shatter him, cause him to disintegrate into a thousand shards, glass-like tears.

The moment passes, and instead of shattering, he mumbles to her: "I'm going upstairs. I need the toilet. Perhaps a shower, before . . . Give me a few minutes. I'll call you up when I'm ready." His voice wobbles a bit. "Here's your tea."

He shoves the mug into her hands, and almost runs out of the room. She hears him pounding up the stairs.

She sits down on the sofa, sips the tea, rubs her head. The headache's getting worse.

And wonderful games to play . . .

Oh, shurrup, shurrup, shurrup, she says to her own head. For fuck's sake, shurrup. What a dumbass tune to get stuck in there.

She stands up, wanders about, sits back down. Looks at her watch. For fuck's sake, how long's he going to be, she wonders. Let's hope bitch-wife doesn't come back early. She'll get a shock.

Lisa looks up at the ceiling: she can hear footsteps, shuffling, something heavy being moved. She glances at her watch again. He still doesn't call her up. Fuck's sake.

She taps her fingers, sips more tea. For fuck's sake.

She gives it another few minutes. For fucketty fuck's sake.

Upstairs, there's a thud, a strange creaking noise,

something breaking. That's it, she thinks, I've had enough. She finishes the tea, puts the mug on the mantelpiece in front of the photo, and steps out of the living room. At the bottom of the stairs, she calls up: "Hey! You ready yet? I can't hang round all fucking day, y'know."

There's no answer. She waits a few seconds, then starts tiptoeing upstairs – wondering why the hell she's tiptoeing. She can't hear any movement, any more noises from upstairs. And the quieter things are on the outside, the louder they seem on the inside: with each step, the 'Teddy Bears' Picnic' in her head gets louder – until, on the landing, she can hardly believe it's not real, that the ice-cream van isn't right in front of her. She feels faint, has to steady herself by holding onto the wall for a few seconds.

At six o'clock their mummies and daddies . . .

The bathroom door, at the top of the stairs, is ajar and the room is empty. In one corner, the shower is drip-drip-ping onto the tiles.

She turns to her right. The next door is shut. She shoves it open, and it rubs against the carpet below with a whooshing noise, as though the carpet were overgrown. The room inside is a mess: ripped cardboard boxes, photos scattered, trodden on, dusty box-files, falling-down shelves, the skeletal remains of broken chairs – and, in the corner, half-buried underneath a box of Law textbooks, are the caged sides of a cot, dismantled.

She pulls the door to, and steps over to the next one. From inside, she can hear a noise she can't quite pinpoint

– somewhere between rocking, whining. It's hard to make it out through the headache-din of 'Teddy Bears' Picnic,' which has got stuck on:

They never have any cares
They never have any cares
They never have any cares . . .

The door is slightly open, but she peers instead through the crack on the other side, between door frame and door. She can see sunlight, dust motes, a double bed . . . and then something which silences – just like that – the ice-cream van in her head, makes her turn away, brings up bile into her throat.

Her head suddenly clear, quiet, Lisa wants to be out of here. She wants to be back home – leaving *him*, this whole mess, to his wife. It doesn't matter if home means holding her mum's ponytail back while she throws up. It doesn't matter if it means washing out smelly glasses, throwing empty bottles into the recycling, mopping the floor where her mum's pissed herself. She'll sit her mum down on the sofa, make them both a cup of tea, milk and one sugar, and eat ice cream – she can afford it tonight – and watch some shitty horror on TV. Together.

She wants to be doing that now. She wants to be at home. She wants to be at home before her dad decides to turn up again.

First, though, she shoves the bedroom door fully open, and steps inside. He's lying on the double bed, crying, rocking backwards and forwards. There's a little blood, and he's surrounded by bits of shattered light fitting. In one hand, he's still grasping the belt with which, a few minutes before, he half-heartedly tried to hang himself.

Lisa steps over to him, prises his fingers apart, and takes the belt. He looks up at her, as if he doesn't recognise her through the tears. "What are you going . . . to do?" he asks, catching his breath between sobs.

"Shurrup," she says. "You're pathetic."

She swivels round, steps over to the window, and opens it, dropping the belt onto the lawn below. He watches her, wide-eyed, uncomprehending, from the bed.

"Thank you," he says, though neither he nor she knows what he's thanking her for.

"Fuck you," she says, and leaves the room – leaves him to it.

She steps across the landing, and trip-traps back down the stairs, all of a sudden feeling strangely buoyant. At the bottom, she reaches inside the man's fleece, which is still hanging on the banister, and fishes out his wallet. She takes five twenties out of it and puts it back carefully. She doesn't hesitate, doesn't feel bad, because she knows what she's going to do with the money. She's going to use it to get the locks changed on their flat.

She lets herself out of Fleece Man's front door and closes it quietly behind her. Skipping down the driveway, she grins, and waves the fan of notes in the face of a passing neighbour. Then she tucks them into her jeans pocket, with the others he gave her earlier.

After the ice cream and the horror movie, she thinks she might text that girl in the park.

Heat Death

MALIK DRAINS HIS pint and stands up.

"Right, off home now. Same time next week?"

Zach nods.

"Okay, see you then." Malik glances at his watch. "What are we like, finishing at 8? More like pensioners than thirty-somethings. Do you remember . . ."

Zach nods again. He *does* remember, so Malik doesn't have to finish the sentence. Instead, Malik buttons up his coat: "Better go and see how the missus is getting on," and leaves The Man in Space.

Zach stays in the armchair. He should go too. He's already got his coat on – though, to be honest, he wears his coat most of the time these days. It's only mid-October, but whether October, July or January, he feels the cold: puts the heating on full, wears three layers when teaching, sleeps in his socks. He shivers at the thought of leaving the pub, going outside.

Still, he *should* go. His wife's expecting him home – has probably put some cold pizza aside from tea – and he has to take his daughter to one of her LAMDA speaking exams early tomorrow. Sunday morning: what a stupid time for a test – as if parents need a weekend, for God's sake. Is it in Stafford or Crewe? He can't remember. Then, when they get back, he has marking to do. Then preparation. Then Monday morning. Then five days of lessons, with the Sword of Damocles, aka Ofsted, dangling over him. Then Friday-night exhaustion. Then Saturday again. Then, then, then.

"God," he sighs, sinking back into the armchair. The chair's so old, so saggy, he feels he might carry on sinking if he's not careful – forever and ever, lost down the back with the coins and fluff.

Resisting the temptation to get lost, he pulls himself up again, and takes his half-drunk pint from the low table in front. He sips it, staring into space.

"G-o-o-o-o-d," he sighs, slowly, slowly, elongating the vowel, so the word sounds like a cross between "God" and "Good."

After a few minutes of sipping, staring and sighing, his eyes refocus, and he sees a half-familiar back sitting at the bar.

Isn't that . . .

He's not sure if it is who he thinks it is – he hasn't seen her here for a few weeks. Or is it months? And her hair looks different – not quite as big, more shaped, dyed a different shade of brown. So he stays where he is, watching her, waiting for her to turn round. Then he'll be able to see her profile.

Perhaps she senses someone staring at her, because eventually she swivels round on the barstool to look at him.

She smiles, he nods, and – to his surprise – she tilts her head to one side, indicating the empty stool to her left.

He gets up with some effort – the armchair is so low – and steps over to the bar. She pats the top of the stool, and he perches on it, next to her.

"Hello, Hope. Long time no see." He tries to smile. "What's new?" There's a strange pause. She doesn't say anything, so he fills the silence: "I mean, I haven't seen you in ages. I just wondered . . ."

She frowns slightly, nods, in a way he doesn't understand. He wonders if he's already upset her in some way – can't for the life of him think why, and she's never struck him as a particularly sensitive or temperamental person. He squirms on the stool; it feels uncomfortable in comparison with the armchair, and he wishes he was back there, on his own, lost in sighs and space.

It's not as if he knows Hope very well. She works (or worked, he's not sure which) in this pub, and has served him drinks for three years of Saturdays – at least till recently. They'd chat about this and that, his daughter, her teenage son, pets, rain, while she pulled his pints, and he waited for Malik. Before he started coming here with Malik, there were fourteen or so years when he hardly saw her, except by chance, in passing. First, there were the four years when he was away at university – she didn't go, wasn't interested, stayed in Stoke; then, back in Stoke, as a newly-qualified Physics teacher in their old sixth-form, he was too busy for pubs; then, later, he was a full-time teacher and (unexpectedly) a new father, too busy for anything. Before all of it, fatherhood, teaching, university, he'd been at high school and college with her, along with Malik and many others – others he now half-keeps in touch with via Facebook, seeing them at Christmas during visits to ageing parents. Only Hope and Malik, from their whole wonderful, funny, crazy year group, are still here, still in Stoke.

A dream-like memory surges up out of it all: a memory of one particular sunny afternoon, on the way home from school, Malik and the other lads laughing – they were always laughing – of Malik pushing him towards Hope – of them both standing red face to red face – of them both giggling, knowing what was coming, knowing the script, as if rehearsing something on stage – of him asking her out to the cinema, or bowling, or something – of her kissing him on the lips – of her winking at his mates behind them, whispering in his ear: "You're fun, Zach, but not till you've grown up a bit" – and patting him on the cheeks, sashaying away, blowing a second kiss over her shoulder – and everything in that moment, the kisses, the whisper, the red faces, seeming so intense, so vivid, even now, over twenty years later.

God, he realises with a shock: that happened over twenty years ago. Four years into high school. He's known Hope for more than two-thirds of his life. Bloody hell. Clearly length of acquaintance is not directly proportional – does in no way correlate – with depth of knowledge.

He looks at her: she's still got the bouffant hair she had at fifteen, even though it seems tamer, less animate than usual; she's still got the large front teeth, big hips. She's still taller than him, still wider than him. Having said that, most people are wider than him: he's never been able to put on weight, never been much more than bone-thin, as his wife puts it, when she tries to cuddle up to him at night. The only thing that's changed much, he thinks, is

Hope's voice: it's softer, slower than it used to be. It sounds lullaby-sad when she finally speaks.

"It has been a long time," she says. "Yes."

"Can I buy you a drink?" he asks, surprised by his own question. He wonders if he's trying to make up for having upset her – though he really can't understand why something so innocuous as "Long time no see" could upset anybody.

"Yes, that'd be nice," she says, nodding, brightening. "It'd make a nice change from me pulling pints for you. Bacardi and Coke, please."

He orders, pays, and while he's waiting for change, says to her: "Are you still working here, then?" He stops himself from adding: "I haven't seen you behind the bar in ages."

"I'm coming back to work, yes. Starting again tomorrow. It feels good getting back to it after being away so long." She mentions the time lapse now without flinching – just glances down at her glass. He wants to ask her where she's been, but doesn't feel he knows her well enough.

Instead, he says: "Glad to hear it," and sips his pint.

There's a pause. "How's your Annie?" she asks. "It is Annie, isn't it, your daughter? And Sara too – how are they both?"

"Both fine," he says. "Trundling along. We're all trundling along. And your son? Sorry –" he rummages around his memory for a moment – "I mean, Ed. How's Ed doing these days?"

"He's doing very well," she says. "Fourteen now. At Trentham High. Our old stomping ground, you know."

"Oh," he says. "Good." He sips his pint, doesn't know what else to say.

"Perhaps," she says, to his relief breaking the silence, "your Annie and him will overlap in a few years. Perhaps they'll both be there at Trentham High at the same time, like us. But then again not like us, because they'll be in different years." She counts on her fingers, then gives up. "I can't do the maths. You can, though. You're good with numbers. Will they overlap at Trentham High?"

"No," he says, straight away. "They won't."

"That's a shame," she says. Then she smiles at him – almost beams – though he doesn't look up, doesn't smile in return. "It was such fun, wasn't it, them days?"

"It *was*," he says, peering at his beer. He wonders why it's so flat, where all the bubbles have gone. Perhaps it's off. "It certainly was."

There's a long pause. Her smile dies down, gives up the ghost. She turns to look up at the TV over the corner of the bar.

"Look," she says suddenly – almost squeals – "look. It's the Lottery results."

He looks up too. "Do you do it?"

"Every week," she says. "You never know. It could be you."

"I suppose not," he says. He shivers. "Perhaps it's time I went. Early start tomorrow. Taking Annie to . . ."

"Oh, not yet, Zach. You haven't finished your drink. Just wait with me while the numbers're called. It's nice to have someone to talk to for a change." She breaks into a smile again. "And to moan at when you don't win anything for the millionth week in a row."

"Okay," he says. They watch the show in silence for a

minute or two. He looks at her from the side. She's sitting up straight, eyes wide, transfixed.

"You don't really think you're going to win, do you?" asks Zach.

"Of course not," she says, without looking round. "But it's fun to dream a bit."

"What would you do with the money?" he asks, for something to say.

"I don't know. Maybe a cruise. Go somewhere hot. Somewhere that's not here or Blackpool. Somewhere different. Take my Ed with me. Give up my flat. Buy a caravan. Go driving across Europe. America. Anywhere!" She takes a deep breath, as if overcome, and asks him in return: "What would you do?"

"I never enter," he says.

She goes back to staring at the TV, eyes reflecting colours. There's applause, a drumroll, a deep bass note on a synthesiser, a close-up of numbered balls jumping up and down, revolving, jostling, in a see-through cylinder. A kind of over-sized Brownian motion, Zach thinks. Perhaps he'll use the image to demonstrate Brownian motion, kinetic theory, even statistical mechanics, to some of his A-Level students.

The first number is being drawn.

"Where's your ticket, then?" he asks.

Distracted, concentrating on the TV, she murmurs: "Oh I think it's in my bag. Or perhaps my coat. Or at home, not sure."

"How can you know you've won if you don't have your ticket?"

"I don't need my ticket. I know the numbers off by

heart: my age, Ed's age, Ed's guinea-pig's age, the number of our flat, number of ex-husbands," she blushes slightly, then adds: "and the number of people I've slept with."

"But it's stupid," he blurts out, before he can stop himself, strangely irritated by her list. "It's stupid, using the same numbers every time. It means the one week you don't enter, they'll probably come up."

"Is that a Physics law?" she asks.

"Of course not. It's Sod's Law."

"You make everything sound like Physics," she says.

"No, I don't," he says – though he knows she's got a point. "All I'm saying is, if you choose the same numbers every week, you'll end up being one of those urban myths. You know, all those stupid stories people tell about the Lottery – about how the one week they didn't enter, or lost their ticket, or the newsagent was closed, that was the one week they'd have won. But didn't."

Meanwhile, the first number has been declared: 35. As the ball rolls into place, the voiceover drones a short history of the number – how many times it has been called over the years, when it was last picked, which famous guest on the show was thirty-five their last birthday.

Hope doesn't say anything – merely leans forward on her stool a bit more. Both she and Zach know how old they are.

The next number is called. It's 14. Hope looks oddly disappointed, and her shoulders sag: "This is what it's always like. It starts well and then . . ."

The next number is called. It's 4.

"How old's Ed's guinea-pig?" asks Zach.

"Four," she says. They both look at the TV.

The fourth number is called. It's 12.

"That's my flat number," says Hope, not moving.

The next number is 2. "Two ex-husbands," says Hope. Zach wonders what the hell is happening.

The final number is called. It's 53. He looks at her, and she looks at him. She grins and bats him playfully on the wrist. "No. How dare you. What kind of girl do you think I am?"

"I've no idea," he says, and – for the first time – smiles back.

They've almost forgotten about the bonus ball, and turn back just in time: 41.

He sips his drink. Then stops. She's still. Very still.

"That's it," she murmurs. "That's how many people – if you count a couple of women – I've slept with."

His first thought is: God, how come she's shocked at the idea of sleeping with fifty-three people, as opposed to forty-one? His second thought is: God, that's thirty-seven more than me. His third thought is spoken out loud: "Bloody hell, Hope. You've won."

The landlord, who's polishing glasses a couple of yards away, looks up. "Really?" he asks. "Are you joshing us, Hope?"

"No, I'm not. I've won." She says it so breathily, so quietly, so intensely that no-one who overhears – not Zach, not the landlord, not the other barmaid, not the two men waiting for drinks at the opposite end of the bar – doubts it again.

"Oh my God, Hope," shrieks the barmaid. She stamps her foot. "Ohmygodohmygodohmygodohmygod."

The landlord is crying. "This is incredible," he wheezes

over and over. After a puff on his inhaler, he manages to say: "I'm so pleased for you, Hope. After everything you've been through." He reaches over the bar and kisses her on both cheeks.

The barmaid, meanwhile, scuttles from her side of the bar and grabs Hope from behind – pulls her off the stool and hugs her, jumping up and down at the same time: "Ohmygodohmygodohmygod." The two men at the opposite end of the bar don't know what to do and are staring open-mouthed.

Zach is looking from TV screen, where they're repeating the winning numbers for the third time, back to Hope's face, back to TV screen: 2, 4, 12, 14, 35, 53, and Bonus Ball 41. He mutters the numbers under his breath, as if they're some kind of curse, spell, Physics equation: 2, 4, 12, 14, 35, 53, 41.

Finally, he slips off the stool, and – for the first time in twenty years – kisses Hope, this time on the cheek. She touches her cheek afterwards, murmuring something about his lips feeling cold. Then he embraces her, gently. "Congratulations, Hope. Who'd have thought it."

The two men have come over too and form a queue to hug her in turn. "Congratulations," one of them slurs. "And if you need any help spending it, darling . . ."

She laughs and pushes him away.

"Get everyone drinks, Frank," she says to the landlord. "A round of shots. And other drinks too – whatever anyone wants. All on me."

While everyone is ordering, she retrieves her handbag from the floor, unclasps it, and starts rummaging inside. The drinks arrive, one by one, and still she's rummaging.

The landlord, who's got tears standing in his eyes, puts his hand over hers: "Hope, don't worry. If you haven't got the cash on you, I'll stand these. They're on the house." He grins. "You'll be able to pay us back with interest in a few days. We'll miss you here, you know."

Everyone takes the shots, clinking them together, saying: "Cheers," toasting Hope, and downing them. Everyone, that is, except Hope. She closes her handbag and looks up.

"What's the matter?" asks Zach, wiping his mouth with his sleeve.

"The ticket isn't in my bag." She takes the final shot and downs it. "Cheers," she says to everyone, holding up the empty glass. The others crowd round and jostle to clink their glasses repeatedly against hers – as if, by doing so, some of her good luck might rub off.

"Are you sure?" asks Zach, who's been pushed aside, and is on tiptoes, trying to talk over others' heads.

"Yes," she says. "I checked twice. It's not here."

The glass clinking dies down, and everyone's talking at once: what she should do with the money, where she might visit, what she might eat and drink, where she might invest it, whether property prices in Stoke or down south represent better prospects, and so on. Only Zach is talking to her directly; only Zach hears what she has said.

"Where is it then?"

"It's probably at home. In the flat."

"Probably?" he asks, frowning. "*Probably?*" He feels like shaking her, his tone shot through with impatience: "For God's sake," he wants to say to her, "for God's sake: *probably?*" She doesn't notice, and her tone remains quiet, dreamy.

"Yes, probably . . . No, definitely. I can see it: I must've left it on the worktop. It'll be there when I get home. I can't wait to tell Ed." She opens her handbag again, takes out her mobile, hesitates, puts it back in. "No, I won't call or text him yet. I'll wait till I've got home – till I've got the ticket in my hand. I know: I'll send him a photo of it. Just a photo, with no explanation." She laughs. "He'll wonder what it means, why I've messaged him a photo of a lottery ticket." She imagines her son's face gradually changing, the truth dawning: "And then he'll get it. He'll check the numbers or something on his phone. He'll call me. And you know what? Everything'll be okay again." She turns to Zach, takes his hand. "I can't believe it, Zach. Everything's going to be okay, isn't it?"

He nods. "But you need to find the ticket."

"You're right," she says, slipping off the stool, suddenly decisive, galvanised by the image of her son's face. She points at Zach's pint: "Down that, and we'll go and get it."

"We?" he asks – but she doesn't hear, because she's distracted by the landlord, who puts his hand on her shoulder, over the bar.

"Going already?" the landlord asks, disappointed. No-one except Zach has picked up that she can't find the ticket.

Hope smiles at him, squeezes the hand on her shoulder. "Just for now," she says.

"We could have a lock-in if you like. Special occasion."

"Thanks, Frank. But I want to go home. Tell Ed." She leans over the bar and kisses him on the cheek. Then hesitates, looks him in the eyes, and kisses him full on the lips.

The barmaid whistles, laughs and claps her hands. Zach looks away, tries not to remember – again – what her kiss was like when they were fifteen.

"That's to say thank you, Frank," whispers Hope, holding his cheeks. "Thank you for everything."

She pulls away and starts putting on her coat. Zach helps her.

"Don't forget us," the landlord says. Zach's worried he's going to start blubbing, and wants to leave before he does.

"You can't get rid of me that easily," Hope says, blowing him another kiss, hugging the barmaid tightly, and turning to go. The two men line up, for another drunken hug. She lets them peck her on the cheek. Then she makes for the door.

Zach swallows down the rest of his pint, nods at the landlord and barmaid, and follows Hope, in time to open the door for her. They leave in a flurry of goodbyes: "Goodbye," "Good luck," "Come back soon," "Congratulations," "It's wonderful news," "Couldn't happen to a lovelier person," "Love you," "We'll miss you."

Outside, Zach does up his coat, puts his hands in his pockets. "It's bloody freezing."

"It's not," says Hope. She takes his arm. He wonders if she can feel the body heat escaping through his coat sleeve. He thinks of heat loss, of the laws of thermodynamics, of last week's lessons. She squeezes his arm more tightly, rubs it up and down, as if to warm it up.

"It's not," she says again, "it's a lovely night. So dark – look, the moon's only a lemon slice in a gin." Almost skipping, she pulls him through the streets, down a couple of alleyways, through a subway under the A50, across a

patch of wasteland to a squat block of flats, and finally up
to her flat: Number 12.

◊

Still in his coat, Zach is sitting on Hope's sofa. It's cold,
and he'd like to ask her to put the heating up, but thinks
it might seem a bit rude. He glances round, wondering
why he's here.

The flat is small. To his left is a tiny kitchen area, separated from the living room – where he's currently sitting
– by an island worktop, covered in pans, plates and bills.
Behind him are two closed doors, one to the bathroom
– which he's just visited for a piss – one presumably to
Ed's bedroom. In front of him is an old TV and, next to
it, another door, ajar. Through the doorway, he can see
the bottom half of a double bed, a pink duvet, a blanket
over the window in place of curtains. He looks away,and
sees something in the right-hand corner of the living-room
which, oddly enough, he hasn't noticed before: an upright
piano.

"Do you want a drink?" Hope asks, as she comes out
of the bathroom.

"Shouldn't you be looking for a ticket?" he asks back,
shuffling on the sofa.

"Yeah, but let's get a drink first." She steps over to the
kitchen area, opens a cupboard over the sink, and peers
inside: "I've got gin. Is that okay?"

"Yes. A small one." He thinks about how late it is; how
he really should be at home; how he has to take his daughter to the examination early tomorrow morning; how his

wife will be wondering where he is; how he could text her, but won't. He glances at the half-open bedroom door again.

"I've got some lemonade somewhere, I think. It might be a bit flat . . ." She opens and shuts various cupboards, until the door comes off one and crashes to the floor. "Oh shit," she says. "It's always doing that." She giggles, and retrieves a cheap bottle of lemonade from inside the exposed cupboard. There's nothing else in there. She finds two tumblers on the draining board, and brings everything – gin bottle, lemonade, glasses – over to the coffee table in front of Zach. She sits down next to him on the small sofa. One of her knees touches his. She pours the lemonade into tumblers and tops it up with a good two or three inches of gin. They clink glasses, and drink. She almost drains her glass.

"Are you going to look for the ticket?" he asks.

"In a minute." She's slurring a little.

He shuffles uncomfortably again. He's finding it hard to keep still, with a winning lottery ticket somewhere in the flat. "Aren't you worried? Don't you want to get it sorted?"

"Of course. But I'm sure it's under the papers on there" – she indicates the worktop – "somewhere."

He sips the gin. He looks down and sees her hand resting lightly on his thigh. He must be tipsy, because he hadn't felt her put it there. Her face is close. He can feel the warmth of her breath on his cheek.

"Perhaps we should both hunt for it," he suggests, look-ing away. His lack of arousal worries him. Here she is, here he is, at her place, at night, together. Both sitting on the sofa, together. She's attractive – he finds her attractive, always has. But everything feels cold, and the missing lottery ticket is bothering him: it's somewhere here, just out of reach. "Let's get up and look for it."

She takes her hand away and pouts: "Oh, Zach, you're no fun any more. You used to be, I don't know, *Tigger* and now you're all *Eeyore*. And all teachery-bossy too: look for this, look for that . . ."

"It's not just this or that, Hope. It's a winning lottery ticket, for God's sake."

"I know. But honestly. You used to be a laugh in school. What happened to you?"

"I don't know," he says. There's a pause, and she looks at him sympathetically — as if *she* feels sorry for *him*. It irritates him, and he stands up. For a moment, he thinks about going. How easy it would be to walk out of the flat. Instead, he says: "You go through the stuff on the worktop, and I'll look round the room."

She sighs, finishes her drink and gets up. "Okay then. But promise me you'll stay for another drink when we've got it."

"I promise."

She steps over to the worktop, and starts shuffling through the bills, statements, unopened envelopes, Post-it notes: "I know it's here," she says. "I remember seeing it."

Meanwhile, Zach wanders round the living area, shoving his hand down the back of the sofa, flicking through discarded magazines on the floor, in case the ticket's been used as a bookmark. He works his way round to the piano. He crouches, and flicks through some of the music under the stool: Chopin Études and Nocturnes, Schubert Sonatas, Bach's Preludes and Fugues. He stands and turns to her: "I didn't know you could play."

She looks up at him, across the room: "No," she says, "you didn't."

All too easily distracted, especially by something she loves, she stomps over to the piano, plonks herself on the stool, lifts the lid, and – without any self-consciousness, any inhibitions – hammers out the main theme of Addinsell's *Warsaw Concerto*. She breaks off mid-flow when the next-door neighbour bangs on the wall.

She swivels on the stool to face Zach. He thinks she's crying. "Do you know what that was?"

"No," he says.

"It's the music for an old black and white movie called *Dangerous Moonlight*. I watched it one day when I was off work. It made me cry. The pianist in it's got amnesia from an accident in the war. He's been away from his wife for ages, and can't remember anything, not even her. But the music kind of helps him remember, and they're reunited and everything's okay at the end – well, except for the bombing, the invasion and stuff. It's all so *lovely*," she gushes.

"You must be good, to play stuff like that," he responds, flatly. He doesn't tell her what he thinks of the music, which seems over-blown, naff in this context – in a tiny flat in Stoke-on-Trent, seven decades after the war, with a neighbour banging on the wall. He doesn't tell her that, at this moment, she herself seems over-blown, naff, kitsch. Her intensity irritates him – perhaps because it reminds him of something he's lost, half-forgotten, in a kind of emotional amnesia.

"Anyway, shouldn't we be finding this bloody ticket?" he asks.

She shrugs her shoulders. "I'd rather be playing *Dangerous Moonlight* for you."

"Our Annie's starting to learn," he says, trying to steer the conversation away from *Dangerous Moonlight*.

"I could teach her," Hope says, then adds: "But she's probably already got a teacher." She gets off the stool and returns to the worktop. He moves in the opposite direction, keeping his distance, and starts flicking through music on top of the piano.

"Do you teach as well?"

"A bit," she says, turning over an unpaid BT bill. "It's helped these last few months. When I couldn't manage the job at The Man in Space, at least I could do a bit of teaching here. It helped pay a few of these bills."

He turns around, stares at her. He's drunker now, braver, so is going to ask her outright: "What's been going on these last few months, Hope? Where've you been?" Before he can do so, though, she squeals, and stamps her feet on the floor.

"Got it!" she shrieks, waving a slip of paper. "I knew it was here."

He sighs with relief. "For a few minutes there, I thought . . ."

"I know," she says, "you were worried. But I knew it was here." She waves it again. "Time for another drink."

She brings the ticket over to him, and kisses him on the cheek. "You see – I knew it was okay."

He takes the ticket, and glances down at it – trying not to be jealous, trying not to think of all the things he could do, if this small, half-screwed-up piece of paper were his.

Yes: the numbers are all there: 2, 4, 12, 14, 35, 41.

"You've done it, Hope," he whispers. "Congratulations."

He's about to pass the ticket back to her, when the date at the bottom comes into focus: SAT 19 SEPT.

She reaches out for the ticket and takes hold of the top of it between thumb and forefinger. He doesn't let it go, and it's taut between them.

"What?" she asks. She raises an eyebrow: "Don't you want to give it to me, Zach?"

"It's not the right one," he says. "It's a September ticket." He lets it go, and she takes it, turns it round, peers at it. She's clearly having difficulty focussing.

"Oh." She drops the ticket, and it falls, drifting from side to side like a feather, till it lands at their feet.

He looks down at it, then back up at her: "*Oh?*" he says, "*Oh?* Is that all you've got to say? *Oh?*" He's holding her arms, trying not to shake her: "For God's sake, Hope."

"Stop it." She pulls away, turns her back on him. He thinks she's going to start searching for the ticket again. He's wrong. "I tell you what," she says over her shoulder. "Let's get another drink, have a sit, then we can start hunting again." She plumps herself down on the sofa and pats the space next to her. He stares at her, open-mouthed, a statue.

She waits for him a few seconds. When he doesn't move, doesn't respond, she says: "Suit yourself," and reaches for her glass.

As she's pouring herself some lemonade, spilling a bit onto the table, he comes back to life: "For Christ's sake, Hope. Somewhere in this flat is two million quid, or whatever. We need to find it. *You* need to find it." She carries on making her drink – pouring the gin. He breathes out, almost hissing: "Okay then. I'll find it for you."

He stomps over to the worktop, and starts going through the papers: ordering them, putting them into piles. Now and then he comes across a smaller piece of paper: a receipt, or an old lottery ticket. These he glances at, and discards. "No, not here," he mutters.

He turns and starts opening and banging shut cupboards. "For God's sake, Hope," he keeps muttering, growling, "where the hell did you put it?"

"I can't quite remember," she says from the sofa, where she's enjoying her drink. "Why don't you come and j . . ."

"No. I'm going to find it if it kills me."

He opens one cupboard above the cooker, and dozens of receipts, bank statements and bills rain down on him. He stoops to pick some of them off the floor. "Bloody hell, Hope, how can you find anything in this mess?"

"Why's it so important to you?" she slurs from the sofa. "It's *my* ticket." She pauses. "It's mine, you know, to lose if I like."

"Oh, shut up." He's sweating now, desperate, sorting through papers, peering in the cupboard, scraping a stool over from the worktop so he can perch on top, get a better look – then giving up on this cupboard, opening and shutting others, returning to the worktop, riffling through the piles he's just made – then, his frustration spiralling exponentially, scattering the piles of papers on the floor – then back in the living area, hurling magazines around, shoving his hands down the back and sides of the sofa, leaning over Hope ("Ooh, Zach, that feels nice, you can keep rummaging there if you like . . .") – then attacking the piano stool, throwing Chopin, Schubert and Bach around ("Not my music, Zach, *per-lease*") – then almost running to the son's bedroom, storming into it, ready to tear it to pieces – where is it? where is the damn ticket, for God's sake, where is it? – until he's confronted by such tidiness, such near-emptiness, he comes to a standstill. The bed is well-made. There's nothing on the floor. There's nothing on the desk, on the chest of drawers. He opens the tiny wardrobe, and finds only rattling hangers, one set of neatly-folded pyjamas at the bottom. There's nowhere to search in this room, because everything is in its place or gone – and that takes the wind out of his sails. He stops, frowns.

Panting, he steps back into the living room. He reaches up to the wetness on his face, thinking it's sweat. He flashes back to the question she'd asked a few minutes ago: "Why's it so important to you?" He doesn't know, has no idea why finding someone else's lottery ticket is so important to him.

Instead of trying to answer the question, he asks another: "Why is Ed's room so . . . tidy?" Zach catches his breath, thinking for a second she's going to say that he's died. Perhaps that's why she's been away from work. "Where is he?"

"He's at his dad's."

Exhausted, trembling, Zach steps back to the sofa, and sinks down next to her. She puts her hand on his arm, offers him a drink she's got ready for him.

"Here. I think you need this."

"I thought Ed lived with you," Zach says.

"He did, till four months ago. He moved in with his dad and stepmum for a few weeks, you know, when things were so up in the air. He took his guinea-pig with him." She speaks slowly, carefully, picking her way through emotional rubble. "He decided to stay on for a bit afterwards – after things settled down. They've got a nicer house, more money." She grins. "Or, if we find that ticket, they *had* more money."

She tops up her drink with more gin. "I miss him, you know. And his guinea-pig."

Zach asks her directly now: "What things have been up in the air, Hope? What's been going on? Why haven't you been at The Man in Space?"

She smiles at him. "I've just had . . . a touch of cancer." She reaches behind herself, unclips her bra, and starts pulling up her top.

"I'm not . . ."

"Shhh," she says, putting a finger on his lips, slipping her bra down.

For a moment, he wonders what he's looking at. The left breast next to him is full, bell-like, what he expected. The right side is a scarred space, as if the breast has come off with the bra – which, in a way, it has.

She sits there, unembarrassed, an eyebrow raised. "They're going to operate again in a few weeks. Reconstruction, they call it. They couldn't do it at the same time as they cut it off, because of the radiotherapy." She tugs at her hair: "Don't worry, I'm not going to take this off too." He frowns, confused. "You didn't think it was mine, did you? Didn't you even notice it looked different? God, *men*."

He nods and shakes his head at the same time, staring down once more at her chest. She smiles at him, almost pityingly, licks her lips: "You can touch it if you like." He doesn't move. "Only if you want to, of course."

He still doesn't move. "I had no idea."

"I thought you already knew," she says, "at least till you asked me in the pub what I'd been up to. You confused me, Zach – I wasn't sure if you didn't know, or if you did know and had forgotten, or if you were taking the piss somehow. And after, well, I couldn't be bothered telling you. There's always so many people to tell. It gets boring. Tiring. Tonight's the first time I've had some fun without anyone asking me about it."

He's still staring at the space where a breast used to be. "There seems to be a lot I don't know about you – about everyone," he says, and shivers. She thinks he's shivering at her, with a kind of horror, repulsion. She pulls down her top, starts doing up her bra.

But he's not shivering because of her. He's shivering because he feels cold. He's shivering because he feels that all the heat in his body, in the flat, in the universe is draining away – no, *dispersing*. That's it, he thinks: he's shivering because of heat dispersal. He's shivering because of the Second Law of Thermodynamics, which he was teaching, only last week, to a group of Gifted and Talented students: "The Second Law states that the entropy of an isolated system increases over time – that heat will always transfer from a hotter body to a colder one – that this process is not spontaneously reversible – that therefore the universe must be expanding, dispersing and cooling from a point of infinite heat, infinite density – that eventually, after roughly 10^{100} years, the logical end-point of the Second Law suggests that the universe will attain thermodynamic equilibrium, a state of maximum entropy, *heat death*, where temperatures are levelled-out, energy dissipated, particles dispersed, equidistant from one another, cold . . ." He's shivering because of that cold – because he feels an entropic process operates not only on a universal scale, but on a microcosmic one too, in individual human lives: that people he knew have dispersed like particles, that his own life has moved from a point of almost infinite heat to . . .

He stands up. "I'm sorry. I can't."

She's visibly trembling, her cheeks red.

"It's not that I don't want to." He knows he's hurt her, but doesn't know how to explain himself. "It's just that I'm cold."

"You are," she murmurs. "You really are."

"I've got to go home. My wife. My daughter. You know how it is. I can't."

She doesn't allow herself to cry. Instead, she breathes in deeply, takes his hand, stands up, and they step over together to the front door.

At the door, they face each other. She kisses him on the lips – for the first time since they were fifteen. "We could've been great," she murmurs. "If I'd said yes that afternoon at school. It could've been all romantic like *Dangerous Moonlight*: you and me, the piano, black and white." She chokes something back. "Things would've been different."

He remembers the irreversibility of the Second Law, of heat dispersal: "No, they wouldn't."

He turns to leave, then turns back one last time: "Do you think you'll find the ticket?"

"I don't know." She smiles at him. It's almost as if she doesn't care, he thinks. And that thought is probably the closest thing to love he will ever know.

Bubble Man

THE SQUARE IS full of bubbles. Bubbles everywhere. His daughter is dancing among them, as are twenty or so other children.

The children swarm round the man making the bubbles, who's using a bent coat-hanger on a stick as a wand. He dips the wand into a bucket of suds, then waves it in an arc over their heads, conjuring a bubble-cosmos that swirls, spirals around them. They scatter outwards, the toddlers trying to catch the bubbles, the older children trying to pop them. Some bubbles sail far above their heads, over the shops and town hall, but most are gleefully exterminated.

Then the children are sucked inwards again, round the bubble man, mesmerised as he dips the coat-hanger in the bucket, and waves it over their heads. Again they scatter, dance, giggle – kids and bubbles, all mixed up.

His daughter is giggling too. She's a head higher than most of the children, but is enjoying herself as much as them. She lifts up one toddler, who's tripped over, to help him catch a particularly big bubble. It pops, of course, and both she and the toddler laugh – almost hysterically, it seems to her dad. Until five minutes ago, she hadn't laughed, or even smiled once, all afternoon. She'd hardly said a word – apart from to whinge that the film was crap, the popcorn too chewy, salty. Now she is laughing, chattering with strangers, full of energy rather than yawns and frowns.

Her father watches as bubbles eddy past her, reflecting, refracting her profile, trapping her image in their rainbows. Then they float skywards, taking their miniature versions of her with them, out of his reach.

"It's time to go," he yells at her. She doesn't hear – or pretends not to. If they're late back to her mother's, he knows he'll get another one of those bastard emails from the solicitor: *Dear Mr Strawson . . . under the terms of the . . . your wife . . . custody . . . concerned . . . court order . . .* and so on. "Fucking hell. Cassy, it's time to go!"

She still doesn't pay any attention. Some stuck-up-bitch-mother to his left frowns and tuts at him, his language. He ignores her. *For fuck's sake,* he mutters.

All the children are weaving around one another in complex patterns, aiming for different bubbles. Cassy's father circles the crowd, shoving past stuck-up-bitch-mother and a few other parents on the fringe, shadowing his daughter, ready to catch her. He passes close to bubble man, who stinks. His hair's greasy, his coat shabby, his face streaked with filth. Probably hasn't had a bath in weeks, Cassy's father thinks – since he got off the boat from whatever Eastern European shithole he's come from. Only his fingers stand out, sparklingly clean by comparison, from contact with soapy water in the bucket.

Next to bubble man is a shoebox, with a cardboard sign propped up against it. The sign reads:

Pleese give genrusly to help pay for:
my Ferrarree,
my home in Monnaco
& my socks.
Thank u very mutch,
Cristian aka The Pide Piper x.

Cassy's father looks up from the sign at exactly the right moment: there's his daughter, chasing a bubble, a foot away from him. He lunges forward and grabs her arm – before she manages to reach the bubble – and pulls her out of the swirl of bubbles and children. "Hey!" she says, looking down at his hand. "That hurts." He doesn't let go.

"Come on. I've gotta get you back to your mother."

She frowns, her eyebrows dark against her face, as if it's his fault they've got to go. As if *any* of it is his fault.

"Look, Cassy, we've got to go. It's not my bloody fault. You know what they're like, your mother and *Derek*." He says the name like it's swearing.

"At least Derek'd let me stay here a while. At least Derek doesn't take me to a film for five-year-olds. At least . . ."

"It's not my fault," he says, through clenched teeth.

He half turns, and starts pulling her after him. She staggers a bit, and trips over bubble man's shoebox and sign. She wrenches her arm free – her father is surprised how strong she is these days – and kneels down, to right the sign.

She holds the sign in front of her and reads it out loud: *Please give genrusly to help pay for . . .*

Her forehead's creased for a moment after she finishes reading it – and then she grins: "It's a joke, isn't it, Dad? He hasn't got a house or Ferrari, has he? He's joking because really he's poor."

"That's what he wants you to think."

She stands up, faces her father. "I think we should give him some money," she says. "He's fun." Her father wonders if she's about to add: *unlike you.*

"You must be kid . . ." but he trails off, realising she isn't. She's staring directly at him, into his eyes, for the first time since – well, for weeks. Her eyes are quivering like bubbles. She looks like his little girl again.

"Please, *Dad*. It was fun. The nice man deserves it. He's poor and he made me laugh."

Cassy's father reaches into his jeans pocket, pulls out his wallet. He knows there's probably not much in there. Today's cleared him out for a few days. He's got about five pounds left either for The Bitter End – his local – or food. He hasn't decided which yet.

He opens up his wallet. She's watching, peering inside. There's the lone five-pound note. He unclips the pocket for change. There are two coins – 5p and 1p.

He hesitates. She's still watching. He takes out the two coins, offers them to her.

"You can't just give him that," she says. "That's nothing." She reaches over and pulls out the five-pound note.

"Cass . . ."

"It was worth it," she says. "Much better than the film, and that cost more." She kneels down and puts the note into bubble man's shoebox. Her father's mouth opens and closes.

Cassy stands up, turns her back on him, and flounces off. He glances down at the shoebox, wondering if he can get away with reaching down to retrieve the note, without his daughter noticing. But he's worried that she'll turn round, see him do it – and, at the same time, that he's about to lose sight of her in the crowd. So he runs after her, pushing people out of the way, swearing at them.

He catches up with her. She doesn't look at him – doesn't thank him for giving all his cash to a stinking Romanian, gippo, pikey, whatever he is, doesn't thank him for the afternoon, won't kiss him goodbye when they get back to her mother's place, will merely slouch in, grunt something, and Derek'll shut the door in his face – and then, without any money, he won't even be able to go and whinge about fucking ex-wives, fucking stepfathers, fucking lawyers to whoever will listen at The Bitter End, will just be on his own.

Still, he could always call up a few of his EDL mates, tell them there's a kiddy-fiddling-Romanian-pikey in town, and they can go and do him over. Stick his bubbles where the sun don't shine. Make him eat his stupid sign, his own words: *Ferrari, Monaco, socks*. At least then the day won't have been a total write-off.

Trial

Notes by Mr Keith McNamara
FAO Dr Christopher Sollertinsky, St. B———— Hospital

Day 1
Today I was my husband's dead mother.

Day 2
Today I was the milkman – or the milkman was imper-
sonating me. Or something like that. I'm not entirely sure.
I mean, we don't even have a milkman.

Day 4
Today I was my husband's dead mother again. I tell you,
Doc: Freud would have a field day in this house.

Day 8
Today, Doc, I was his long-dead mother *again*. Yawn: it's
getting boring now. A tale told by an idiot.

I said to him: it's me, *Keith*, your husband. I held his face
between my hands, made him look straight at me. He said:
no it's not. It's not you. It's not Keith. It's mother, pretending

to be you. He shook his head over and over, shouted: I don't know why she – why *you* would do this to me. I don't know why you've come back. I don't understand. I never bloody well understood you when you were alive, let alone now.

Then he backed off down the hallway, kept glancing from side to side, terrified. When he was a kid, all those decades ago, his mother used to lock him in the downstairs toilet – shove him in, turn the key on the outside – every time he told her he wanted to be an actor, not a doctor or teacher or accountant. She didn't care about him being gay, just his earning potential. This afternoon, he thought *I* was going to do that to him – he thought *I* was going to lock him in the toilet.

What's happening to him, to us, Doc? Where's this leading? At this rate, we're all going to end up trapped in a downstairs toilet, scrabbling around in the dark, like some never-ending Beckett play. Waiting for the real me to reappear.

Day 10
Today – well, today, Doc, I couldn't work out *who* I was supposed to be.

Look here, I'm doing what you asked. You asked me to keep a record of what happens, who he thinks I am, day to day. You asked me to write everything down during 'the trial' – everything and anything that might be relevant – so you can chart if his delusions are improving or getting worse. But sometimes it's difficult to know what's happening. Sometimes it's hard to put things into words. And sometimes I think I'm not anyone in particular to him, just some generalised baddie, a body-snatcher, an alien, a crap copy. A photocopy of someone's bottom, as it were. *I am such a tender ass, if my hair do but tickle me, I must scratch . . .*

. . . And sometimes I seem to be lots of people at once, my face ever-changing: Bottom or Banner or Jekyll stuck forever in their transformation scenes.

Day 11

When this trial began, Doc, you told me I'd have to be patient. Wait and see what happens, you said. It might take some time, you said. You said he's got some kind of "Delusional Misidentification Syndrome," which makes recognising faces difficult; I memorised all the names you used, Doc, like a script, so I could google them afterwards. I've never found it hard to learn lines, reciting them *sotto voce* wherever I am, whatever I'm doing: *Capgras, Fregoli, Intermetamorphosis, Capgras, Fregoli, Intermetamorphosis, Capgras . . .*

You said my husband's condition seems to mingle symptoms from all three syndromes, so it's hard to pin it down, reach a "definitive diagnosis." You said, Doc, he was a unique case, fascinating, and you'd like to write a research paper for *The Lancet* about him, his condition, and "possible pharmacological treatments." You said he gets faces mixed up, and he recognises me and doesn't recognise me at the same time. Thinks I'm not me. Thinks someone is impersonating me, or I'm impersonating someone else, or someone's impersonating me impersonating someone else. Who the hell knows?

You said, Doc, it's all because of a damaged "dorsal pathway" to the facial processor. You said the damage might be caused by Lewybodies, the L-Dopa he takes, or it might even be the ECT he had as a boy. You said these things move, so to speak, in mysterious ways – more things in heaven and earth, *et cetera et cetera*. You showed me the MRI scan, and I said I didn't understand. You said that my not understanding was understandable.

Then you said, Doc, that we should trial an "antipsychotic called risperidone" and a "selective serotonin reuptake inhibitor" called citalopram – and that I should write everything down. Keep a day-to-day diary of what happens. You told me I should try and record it all factually, objectively, because it would help you with your research paper. That's what you said, Doc, and I'm trying my best. But, well, my dear fellow, you've got to expect a bit of elaboration and melodrama from two ageing *luvvies*, after all.

And speaking of melodrama, Doc, I don't feel the trial's working.

Day 12
Today I was no-one else, just not-me. He said I looked like me, had the same jawline, complexion, greying nasal hair, but he could tell I wasn't the real me underneath the skin. *I do desire we may be better strangers*, he screamed at me. I always said his Orlando was a bit OTT.

When we met last time, Doc, you told me that this Delusional Misidentification thingymajig, this *cursèd affliction* that makes me a stranger to him, is due to a "disconnection between facial identification and emotional response," between the "temporal lobe and the limbic system," or something like that. My husband, he can identify my features, knows logically who I am, but doesn't *feel* anything – so he assumes I can't be the genuine article, the *bona fide* me. To him, I am merely skin, surface, Shakespearean disguise: my Orlando can see I look like me on the outside, but feels nothing towards the Rosalind inside, as it were. That's your explanation, anyway.

But *why* doesn't he feel anything, Doc? Why, when we have loved each other so intensely, when we are all each other has? When I have never locked him anywhere but in my arms? Has everything between us been acting, impersonation, a sham, hamminess?

And, more than anything, I keep wondering: is Juliet wrong when she asks: "What's in a name? That which we call a rose / By any other name would smell as sweet"? Is she lying, Doc? *He* calls me other names, and then no longer seems to love me.

Day 16

Today, I was his dead mother again. Or, rather, I was a rival actor *playing* his dead mother – cruelly pretending she was still alive. He tried to hit me, Doctor. Tried to lock *me* in the downstairs toilet.

The wheel is come full circle; I am here.

Day 19

This afternoon, I was a girl called Sandy. I'd never even heard of a girl called Sandy. He never told me about her, Doc. He's never spoken to me about exes, let alone *hetero* exes. He put his hand on my knee while we were watching an old *King Lear* of his on VHS – while Gloucester was getting his eye gouged out. It wasn't very erotic. He kissed me and said we should go upstairs. I said okay, but that I wasn't Sandy.

Upstairs, I thought he might get a bit of a shock when I took my trousers off. But he didn't seem surprised at all – as if the lower part of my body has nothing to do with the upper part, if you see what I mean. As if Cesario and Viola might both be real, simultaneously.

He took a selfie of us in bed afterwards, cuddling and smoking. This evening, I found he'd posted it on Facebook, tagging a woman called Sandy in place of me. I didn't know he was friends with her, or any of his exes.

To be honest, I'm scared, Doc. I'm finding things out about his past I never knew. I have no idea what I'll find out next. I thought an illness like his would cover things up, not let them out. It all seems like an undiscover'd country from whose bourn I am scared neither I nor he will ever return.

Day 20
Some days, Doctor, I feel blurry round the edges.

Day 23
Today, I'm apparently a bad imitation – who he can see right through – of Mel Gibson playing Hamlet. I'm some-one playing someone playing someone. Badly.

Day 24
Today, for a little while, I was me again. Perhaps you're right after all, Doc, and the risperidone stuff *is* finally working out. We even had a laugh about his delusions. He called me Keith. He called me *Keith*, for goodness sake.

Then he said sorry for everything, and I said: it's not your fault.

We were sitting outside on the deckchairs in our 'unweeded garden,' even though it was cold. We drank lots of gin (I know you won't approve, but what the hell), and he said now he'll never get to play the Dane. I asked him why not, and he said to me: "How can I, when the faces of Polonius, Laertes, Ophelia, might all get mixed up on stage? Or I might get the actors mixed up with who they're playing – or I might stab one of the audience members by mistake, thinking he or she is Claudius. Who knows?"

I said I wondered if Hamlet himself had a touch of Capgras: after all, he stabs Polonius by mistake, is ghastly to Ophelia, and almost rapes his own mother. Hamlet, I said, can't even recognise clouds, for Christ's sake.

We both laughed for the first time in weeks, Doc, and looked up at the sky, drunkenly, from our deckchairs. Then we slurred our way through the cloud scene – he as Hamlet, me as Polonius. His memory for lines never seems to fail him. Whilst everything else crumbles away, other people's words come back to him whole:

HAMLET: Do you see yonder cloud that's almost in shape of a camel?
POLONIUS: By the mass, and 'tis like a camel, indeed.
HAMLET: Methinks it is like a weasel.
POLONIUS: It is backed like a weasel.
HAMLET: Or like a whale?
POLONIUS: Very like a whale.
HAMLET: Then I will come to my mother by and by. They fool me to the top of my bent.

Afterwards, we held hands, as if we might get up for a final curtain call and bow to our Ophelian audience of weeds and flowers.

Day 25
Sic transit gloria mundi: yesterday, I thought the medicine might be working. Today, I was back to being no-one – back to square one, to Go, *sans* £200, *sans* teeth, *sans* eyes, *sans* everything, as it were. He didn't seem to know me at all, Doc. Shut the door in my face. Asked me why I was in his house. I was a blank to him, a walking silhouette. Polonius behind the arras.

Day 26
He looked in the mirror this morning, Doc, and didn't even know himself.

Day 30
Today, Doc, I was a cat called Caliban. His beloved child-hood pet.

Day 35
This afternoon, Doc, I was long-dead – a great-grandfather he can't ever have known. I felt like a ghost, and he was my medium. He'd summoned me from beyond the veil, and I had nothing to say, no-one to demand vengeance on. Nothing except: "Do you want a slice of lemon with your G&T?" Perhaps there is nothing else left to say.

Day 37
Today, I don't know who I am. I have to be honest, Doc:

I don't know if I can go on with the trial. I think we need rosemary for remembrance, not risperidone.

Day 39?
Today, Doc, I was no-one and everyone – his father, his mother, Sandy, the milkman, Caliban the Cat, Mel Gibson, a great-grandfather, the ghost of Hamlet's father, Horatio. I looked at myself in the cabinet mirror in our downstairs toilet, Doc, and tried to see what he sees, tried to imagine it. I saw faces passing across my own like clouds across sky.

Day – oh, I don't know. I've lost count.
Today, Doc, I was tears, nothing else. They all reflected me, in pieces.

Day – tomorrow and tomorrow and tomorrow . . .
This morning, he shoved me in the downstairs toilet, locked the door from the outside, left me there for two hours. After a while, I gave up calling for help, and studied my reflection again. I didn't understand what I was seeing, couldn't make any sense of it.

I smashed the mirror, Doc, with my face still in it.

Adagietto

For Rowland Cotterill

> They spun webs around me like spiders . . . But I
> am to blame too. Why did I let it happen? My life
> has all been paper!
>
> — GUSTAV MAHLER

I VISITED THE elderly gentleman who called himself
Dr Gustav Mahler, of 22 Woodside Grove, Hanford,
Stoke-on-Trent, only twice.

The first time, in June 1999, I was sent by the Potteries
Official Phonographic Society (POPS for short). "We're
told on the gramophone grapevine he has a remarkable
collection," said the Chairman of the Society. "We've been
trying to gain access to it for years, but he won't talk to any
of us on the committee. He thinks we think he's mad." The
Chairman shrugged his shoulders. "And I think what he
thinks we think is probably spot on. But he doesn't know
you, might trust you, as a new member of the Society."

I frowned, wondering why the Chairman and committee were so fixated on gaining access to this man's collection.

The Chairman noticed my frown, and opened his hands: "Look, I'll be honest with you. We're driven by intellectual curiosity here, of course, but also, shall we say, by more pragmatic motivations: we understand that Dr Mahler – as he calls himself – has no known relatives, or close friends. So, when he dies, as he inevitably must at some point in the future, especially if, as he claims, he really is 139 years old" – here, the Chairman snorted a fake laugh, among half a dozen other sub-clauses – "well, at that point, the collection will have to go somewhere. And we don't want that somewhere to be the wrong hands, or, God forbid, the tip – if, that is, the collection turns out to be worth saving. So we need to ascertain what he has squirreled away up there, in Hanford. As our newest (and very eminent) member, we thought you might like to take on this perfectly benign reconnaissance mission."

◊

It made total sense, of course, that it was I whom the Chairman asked to take on the "mission." Over the years, I'd built up quite a national, maybe even international reputation – if I do say so myself – for my record and music book shop, Scores & Shellac (you might have heard of it). The shop had been mentioned as a 'musical treasure trove' in the *Guardian*, even *The New Yorker*; and everyone in the business knew me as the dealer who could find anything. Everyone knew that, if they wanted a particular classical record, musical biography, score, however obscure or forgotten, I was the person to approach. In my time, I'd arranged for suppressed Soviet Melodiya LPs to be smuggled through the Iron Curtain; I'd traced lost scores by a Norwegian composer whose house had burned down, incinerating most of his life's work; I'd recovered a hitherto-unknown film reel of the Theresienstadt ghetto orchestra playing *Entartete* music, SS officers standing by, grinning, applauding. There was nothing – I thought, and my customers thought – that I couldn't trace. If it existed, I would find it, even if it took years, even if the customer didn't want it any longer. And I did it all, or almost all, from my desk in the shop, telephoning, letter-writing, searching through catalogues and archives.

In the end, perhaps, I'd got a little bored. The internet started to make things simpler – too easy, too accessible – and my customers seemed to lose interest too. The shop started losing money, filling up with books, scores, records which they'd requested, but never bothered to collect. No-one seemed as excited about rare records any more. Everything seemed so damned *available*.

Then my mother died, and I inherited her house. I sold the shop and most of the stock, put the rest in storage, and moved back to Stoke – nearly thirty years after moving away. I'd intended to carry on the business through mail order, even (God help me) experimenting with internet selling; but had hardly done anything on either score when, a few weeks in, I was buttonholed by the Chairman of POPS about Dr Mahler. I can't lie: I was excited; curious. He'd given me something new to do.

Before seeing Dr Mahler in person, I decided to try and find out as much about him as possible. Thankfully, I had a gossipy friend in the next street but one, Sylvie Shelley, of Spark Close, Hanford. I'd known her since school. We'd kept in touch – or, at least, she'd kept in touch with me – even during the three decades I'd been away from Stoke, too busy to think much of anyone back home. Unlike other people roundabouts, Sylvie had never once lectured me about neglecting her or my mother; and all through the funeral and upheaval of moving, she'd helped in small ways – sorting out the garden, recommending plumbers. Everyone seemed to know her, everyone seemed to trust her.

So I trusted her too, and felt I could ask her anything. I called her up, and she seemed happy to hear from me, and told me all she knew.

Dr Gustav Mahler, she said, lived alone. He'd moved to Hanford from somewhere down South three years before, following a family bereavement or divorce or nervous breakdown. He spoke with a comic German accent – or so Sylvie claimed – "like something off *Fawlty Towers*." He was perfectly harmless, but most definitely *mad*, thought my friend. "I get on with him, whenever I see him in the grocer's, or on Neighbourhood Watch business. Apart from being a lunatic, he's a very nice old gentleman."

I asked about his name. Sylvie said his name really was Gustav Mahler: she'd heard from a friend, who'd heard from someone at the Council, that he'd changed it from Dr Egon Young via Deed Poll, a few years previously.

"So, in a sense, he really *is* Gustav Mahler," I said. "Just not the famous one who wrote ten symphonies. A North Staffs Mahler."

"You see, that's what happens to people," she said to me, "whenever they come across him."

"What?"

"They get sucked in. They start believing him, bit by bit. First his name, then other stuff. I've felt it myself."

"What do you mean?"

"I mean, it's like he's so convinced himself, he kind of convinces others round him too."

"You don't mean people actually believe he's a dead composer?"

"No – not quite. Not really. Not if you ask them outright. Then, of course, everyone knows it's nonsense. What I mean is that people always start by saying 'Y'what?' or 'What's he on about?' or 'Who?' when he goes on about symphonies and conducting. A lot of people round here haven't heard of Mahler, and when they realise this guy thinks he's some famous dead musician, they're disappointed it's not Elvis. That's how it is at first: bewilderment and disappointment. But then, over time, their attitudes change – I've seen it myself. The same people who said 'Y'what?' start nodding, smiling at him, as if he's talking sense. And they're not just putting it on. It's like you have to go along with it, like you get sucked into his delusions. He kind of draws you in, like gravity or something."

"He sounds fascinating," I said. "I would very much like to experience this gravitational pull of his. Will you come with me when I visit him? I know you're busy, looking after your sister and all, but it might help me. You can chat to him about Neighbourhood Watch-y things, locks and alarms and so forth, while I root around his collection. In fact, rather than any awkwardness about the Society, we could both pretend to . . . I mean, we could both *be* Neighbourhood Watch people for the day, as it were." There was a silence on the line. "If, of course, you didn't mind."

"I don't think I'm meant to be a party to spying, as Neighbourhood Watch co-ordinator," she said.

"I thought that was the whole point of it," I said.

She couldn't really argue with that, so she laughed half-heartedly, and then sighed: "Okay, then, just this once. You know I'd do anything for you."

This time I laughed; but I don't think she heard, because she'd already put down the receiver.

◊

Next morning, I stood with her as she knocked at the door of 22 Woodside Grove. A shrivelled man with thick round glasses and static hair answered. "Can I help you?" he asked. I did my best not to laugh at his German accent, which really did sound like a '70s British sitcom, or bad war movie.

"Hello, Dr Mahler," said Sylvie, holding out her Neighbourhood Watch identity card. "I think you know me. I've been asked by the local police force to visit people and ask about their household security." She pulled out a clipboard from under her arm: "A quick survey." Dr Mahler didn't say anything, just wriggled, twitched on the spot, seemingly unable to keep still. His eyes kept darting between us, as if he was seeing something we could not.

Sylvie peered round him, into the house: "So if you're free," she asked, "would you mind if we came in for a quick chat?"

Muttering something incomprehensible, Dr Mahler moved to one side, and gestured for us to enter.

The door opened directly into the front room. It was a dingy skip of abandoned meals, unwashed vests, books, scores, and dusty heaps of records and phonograph cylinders – a musical compost heap. Any furniture had long since been buried alive. Dotted here and there among the ruins were classic gramophones: the Columbia Eclipse, Columbia BF Peerless, HMV 28, HMV 31b, Victor 2 Hunchback, Edison Bell Elf, Baby Monarch. I stepped into the room, and their horns surrounded me, like so many iron vortexes, a scrapheap of black holes. I thought I might get sucked in.

"What a collection," I said, before I could stop myself.

"You like, no?" said Dr Mahler.

"I like," I said, hoping he didn't suspect anything.

I needn't have worried, because his attention was distracted by Sylvie, who'd tripped over a couple of books. He gallantly rushed over to her, and guided her through the mess by the arm: "I am sorry for the mess," he said, "but my life, it has all been paper."

I'd heard that expression somewhere before, I thought.

"Shall we go into the kitchen?" asked Sylvie, trying to extract her arm. Having done so, she brandished the clipboard: "Perhaps there we can sit down, and go through these questions about your household security."

He nodded, and she followed him through a trail in the debris to a door on the left. Dr Mahler didn't seem to notice I wasn't following – seemed to have forgotten me. Before Sylvie disappeared into the kitchen after him, she turned and held up five fingers: I had five minutes.

I took out my notebook and pencil and began noting down the makes and serial numbers of all the gramophones.

Next, I had a quick glance at the books. Most of them seemed to be unreturned library books, from all over the country, on musical subjects: orchestration, fugue, Wagner's theories on drama, lives of Beethoven, a first edition of Alma Mahler's biography of Gustav Mahler. I flicked through this last book. Every single line on every single page had been meticulously crossed out in red biro, rendering it worthless.

I picked up a few of the thousands of pages of manuscript paper that carpeted everything. As far as I could tell, it was all nonsense. Thousands and thousands of pages, maybe years of work – and it was all dodecaphonic gobble-degook. I let the papers fall back to where they wanted to lie, while black dots and squiggles swam in front of my eyes.

Finally, with (I reckoned) a couple of minutes to spare, I started to dig into the heaps of records. I scooped up hand-fuls of them. A few were LPs and CDs, but the majority were ancient 78s in brown paper sleeves. There were the usual suspects: Caruso singing *I Pagliacci*; Melba singing *La Traviata*; Mengelberg conducting Wagner's *Tannhäuser* Prelude; an album of Toscanini conducting Beethoven's Seventh.

There were rarer artefacts, including a 1929 set of Bach's Double Violin Concerto. The unnamed orchestra – I found out later – probably consisted of members of the Vienna Philharmonic; the two soloists were the famous virtuoso and long-time leader of the Philharmonic, Arnold Rosé, and his daughter, Alma Rosé; the orchestra was conducted by her brother. I slid one of the records from its sleeve, and out fell a crumpled copy of an old photo. The photo, I again found out later, must have been from around 1907, and featured eight greying figures: Gustav Mahler, with his wife, his two daughters, his sister, his brother-in-law Arnold Rosé, his nephew, and his tiny niece Alma Rosé. It was a mausoleum – the future seemed to cast its shadow backwards onto those pictured: shortly after the photo was taken, Mahler's elder daughter, whose nickname was 'Putzi,' died of scarlet fever, and he himself was diagnosed with fatal heart disease; his niece Alma would end up in Auschwitz-Birkenau, leading the women's orchestra, and dying there in mysterious circumstances; Arnold Rosé, her father, died shortly after the war, his heart broken by loss. All of them were dead – well, except perhaps Mahler himself, who, it seemed, was stuck in some kind of bunga-low-limbo in Stoke-on-Trent.

As I was peering at the photo, looking for echoes, or pre-echoes, of the Stoke Mahler's features on faces of composer and family, one of the discs I was holding under my arm slid out of its sleeve, and rolled on its edge along the floor. It looped round one of the gramophones, and finally clattered to a standstill in a corner. I stepped over to it, and picked it up. Assuming it was part of the same Bach Concerto set, I was about to slip it back into the sleeve, when I felt its different weight, its thicker shellac texture. I glanced down at it, and saw its label, white and gold lettering, with a logo of two gold quavers: 'Columbia Phonograph Company, Pat: Specimen: Test Pressing: Not For Sale: 80 rpm.' This label was half-obscured by another sticker on top, like the kind on homemade jam jars. The sticker looked much newer than the record. On it were scribbled words: '*Adagietto*, New York Philharmonic, 1910.' Underneath was a signature: '*Gustav Mahler*,' and a hand-written dedication: '*für meine Almschi*.'

Clearly, this was ludicrous nonsense, as fake as its owner's delusions. Nonetheless, I was intrigued, distracted – so was still staring at it, weighing it up, when I felt breath on my neck: "Why don't you try it?" whispered Dr Mahler, who'd crept up behind me. "Go on, try it."

He didn't seem remotely surprised or annoyed to find me there, holding a dozen of his records; instead, he guided me by the elbow to one of the Columbia gramophones, and prised the record out of my hands. Then he slipped it onto the turntable. He wound up the handle, and the clockwork motor whirred into action, the blackness starting to spin. The turntable was set to 78 rpm, rather than the 80 stated on the record sleeve, but 2 rpm either way wouldn't make much difference. Dr Mahler carefully lowered the needle onto the shellac.

I watched the needle riding the grooves, surfing the warps, the record spinning round and round, drawing me into its crackles – until I felt as if I were orbiting it, rather than watching it rotate. Dr Mahler and now Sylvie – holding her clipboard – stood next to me, similarly mesmerised.

At first, all I could hear was a darkness of crackles, hiss, fuzz, as thick as a forest. Then, from far away, from a deeper darkness, loomed fragmentary sounds of a string orchestra.

The three of us waited and listened.

The orchestra seemed to be murmuring the opening of the *Adagietto* from Mahler's Fifth Symphony – an orchestral love-song, scored for strings and harp, dedicated to the composer's wife, Alma. The acoustic was dry, the orchestra out of tune, the tempo at first too quick, almost cursory, and the cadences merged with the crackles and warps. It was a primitive, acoustical recording, presumably made by a few members of the New York Philharmonic string section crowded round a recording horn, playing Stroh violins – that is, violins amplified with a metal horn. The sound waves from the Stroh violins were sucked down another recording horn, and, through tiny changes in air pressure, vibrated a stylus which etched grooves onto the surface of the disc. The resulting sound was all shrill-treble; there seemed to be little or no bass sound at all. Sometimes, on such early recordings, brass players stood in for 'cellos and double-basses. But here, the melody had no shadow, no depth, and I wondered if the piece had been specially rearranged for Stroh violins and violas alone – an orchestra of *castrati*.

Yet from this orchestra of *castrati*, from this wreckage of crackles and darkness, from this cursory baton-driven reading, from the record's ever-decreasing circles of sound, there gradually emerged the whisper of something – something like a secret, something like a spell, something which made the room go cold, turned us to stone. For a few moments, I wondered if I were going to cry, in a way I hadn't done for decades, not even at my mother's funeral – or if, somehow, the music were crying for me.

After four minutes, though, the side finished before my tears arrived, and before the music had ended. I wanted to hear the rest. So, without waiting for Dr Mahler to say anything, I flipped the record over – but of course it was blank, one-sided. I took it off, then bent down and rummaged through the pile of records by my feet. Eventually, I found one that felt of similar weight and thickness to the first. I slipped it out of its brown sleeve. There was no label on it, no sticker. Still, I was hopeful: it felt, looked, even smelt like the twin of the first disc. I placed it on the turntable, lowered the needle onto the first groove – only to hear nothing this time except crackles, hiss, darkness. I moved the needle on a couple of times, but there was nothing there. The crackles and warps were empty, echoey, the record a deserted concert hall.

Dr Mahler, sensing my disappointment, touched my elbow again: "We never reached the end," he said.

"I don't know what you mean," I said.

"I mean, it was merely a test, one take. We did the first few minutes. The next year, we were going to record the whole movement." He frowned, puzzled by something. "But for some reason I never went back."

"You're telling me," I said, almost coughing, "that that's Mahler – okay, *you* – conducting his . . . your own music?"

He nodded. Behind him, I saw Sylvie tilt her head towards the front door. It was time to leave. "Thank you, Dr Mahler," said Sylvie, shaking his hand. "It was a very useful meeting." She waved a key at him, "And thank you for this, too. Living alone, it's important for your own safety that a neighbour – someone *trustworthy* – has a spare key for emergencies." She nodded her head again towards the front door: she couldn't, wouldn't give me any more time.

I glanced back at the turntable and the records surrounding it. What did it mean? It simply couldn't have been Gustav Mahler conducting his own music. There are no extant recordings of Mahler as conductor. There are piano rolls made by Mahler, which have been transferred onto CD. There's also a (very) dubious piano recording which purports to be Mahler playing Mendelssohn's *Rondo Capriccioso* in 1905. Orchestrally speaking, though, there is nothing; in 1911, he died that bit too early.

So, most probably, the record I'd been listening to was just another of Dr Mahler's delusions, and it wasn't worth dwelling on. I let myself be led back out into the sunshine. I let the door be shut behind me, between the record and myself. I let Sylvie take me for a coffee, and a chat. "Don't dwell on it," she said to me, echoing – as she often did – what I was telling myself.

◊

The problem was, though, that I couldn't help dwelling on it: the music, the crackles, the shrillness haunted me afterwards, repeating over and again in my head – Iike the recording itself, never reaching an end-point or coda, spinning round and round at 78 rpm: *quavers C, D, E to crotchet E, leaning into the tonic, dotted-crotchet F . . . quavers C, D, E to crotchet E, leaning into the tonic, dotted-crotchet F . . . quavers C, D, E to crotchet E . . .*

Meanwhile, I reported back to the Chairman of the Potteries Official Phonographic Society. I told him everything I'd seen, the 78s, the original Alma Rosé records, the beautiful gramophones – everything apart from the *Adagietto*. All the time I was talking to him, I could hear the music in my head; but I didn't tell him about it. I couldn't face the questions, and didn't want him to think I was crazy too.

How could I explain it? I couldn't put it into words: *And, well, I know it's certainly, almost certainly, not the case; I know it's impossible, almost impossible, no, totally impossible; but still, I can't help wondering if what I heard on that record in Dr Mahler's bungalow is some lost echo of Mahler conducting his own music. But no. There were no recordings ever made of Mahler conducting, test pressings or otherwise. It's not possible. And if any of it by any impossible chance were possible, well, of course, we know that Dr Mahler, or whoever he is, would be sitting on a fortune.*

◊

The one person I did tell about my unending mental *Adagietto* was Sylvie. "I thought you looked distracted," she said, "or more distracted than normal, anyway. And you look like you're muttering something under your breath all the time."

"I can't help it," I said, trying to make light of it. "The melody won't go away. To be honest, I'm a bit desperate. I can't concentrate on anything."

"Well, look," she said, "I've got an idea."

That was the thing about Sylvie: she always had an idea, always had an answer to every problem. She was so practical, pragmatic – the opposite, in many ways, of me.

Her idea this time was to talk to her sister's consultant, a neurologist called Prof. Christopher Sollertinsky, at their next appointment. These days, Sylvie was more or less a full-time carer for her sister, so she generally visited the neurologist with her. They'd almost become friends: Sylvie, being Sylvie, baked Prof. Sollertinsky rock cakes, gave him advice on security when his car was broken into, knitted him a scarf for the winter.

"I can ask him something in return for the scarf," she said to me. "He won't mind."

And remarkably, he didn't. Sylvie had that way with her: she could charm mad old composers, overworked consultants, anyone. I could never understand it, never see it myself – whatever 'it' was – and seemed to be the only person who was immune.

"He's going to call you later," she said.

"You could charm anyone," I said.

"I wish that were true," she said, and hung up.

I have no idea why, but the moment she hung up, a memory I hadn't revisited in decades suddenly came back to me: we were in the last year of high school. It was lunch-time, and we were both in the music room – me practising something on the piano for the Christmas concert, her pretending to practise her clarinet. Quite why she bothered was beyond me; she was never any good, just seemed to want an excuse to hang around. It can't have been for the company: I'd hardly speak to her, because I was concentrating hard on the concert piece, rehearsing it, dissecting it, playing individual bars or phrases over and over. Now and then, others would burst in, having escaped from the playground, evaded the prefects.

One afternoon, I remember there were three other boys in the room, knocking over music stands, throwing records everywhere. I was saying, "Please stop" – as much to a strange garish halo that had appeared round them, the piano, the score, as to them. I remember the halo more than their faces – that day was the first time I saw it.

The boys stalked over to me at the piano. "Pleasestop-pleasestoppleasestop," they mimicked me, and slammed the fallboard down, onto my fingers. I can still hear the way the piano's strings groaned in pain. They were about to do it a second time: two of the boys were holding my hands down on the keyboard, and the other boy was getting ready to slam the fallboard onto them. "That'll teach you, spaz," they said. "Now you won't bore us shitless at the concert, you smug git." I closed my eyes – to shut them out, to shut out the weird halo shimmering round them.

Then, from the corner of the room, I heard Sylvie mutter something. I didn't understand what she'd said at first. The boys' attention was distracted for a moment: "Y'what?" they asked. She spoke slightly louder this time, but with a wobble in her speech, not unlike her second-rate clarinet-playing: "Please don't hurt him."

"What's it to you?" they asked. "Are you his tart? His *slag*?"

"No," she said, "but please don't hurt his fingers. If you stop, I'll do . . . something for you in return."

I felt the boys' grip on my wrists loosen.

"What's that?" they asked Sylvie. "What're you gonna do for us?"

"You can . . ." She hesitated – and I remember opening my eyes, peering round the piano, seeing this stumpy young girl lick her lips, trying to copy seductresses she'd seen on TV. "You can . . . you'll find out after PE. At the bottom of the field. I'll show you then."

Why on earth would she do that (whatever 'that' was) for them? I remember wondering at the time. But I don't remember anything else. Shortly after they filed out of the room, I fell off the piano stool, suffering my first seizure. I think Sylvie ran to fetch a teacher, and eventually an ambulance.

Later, when I returned to school, I don't recall thanking her for interrupting the bullying, or for helping me during the fit. I don't remember asking her what happened, if anything, at the bottom of the field. I don't even remember the concert, in which I was able to play because of her intervention. As far as I'm aware, we never talked about any of it – never mentioned the incident again – and I've no idea why it came back to me now, thirty-five years later.

And what was most peculiar about the upsurge of memory was that the piece I saw, heard myself practising in the school music room – the piece I was rehearsing, dissecting for the concert, before the boys burst into the room – was a piano arrangement of Mahler's *Adagietto*. In my mind's eye, my mind's ear, I could see the music on the stand, hear it clearly from thirty-five years before. It certainly wasn't that piece at the time – I can't for the life of me remember what it really was, probably a Chopin Étude or Beethoven Bagatelle – but somehow the *Adagietto* had wormed its way backward, retrospectively infiltrating my memory, like some kind of time-travelling parasite. It was as if it had always been there. I wondered if it was going to start colonising all my memories, an all-encompassing *idée fixe* in hindsight. I couldn't understand what was happening to me, and prayed that Sylvie's neurologist might be able to shed some light on the problem.

◊

Prof. Christopher Sollertsinky phoned me up that same evening, out of hours. We talked about the problem for a while, and he told me I was suffering from what's called an "earworm, or *Ohrwurm* in German" – a "catchy tune, or musical meme that won't go away, and which you experience as real, over and over. You are suffering, my friend, from *repetunitis*. You have heard something so profoundly disturbing or striking or suchlike that it has rerouted your neurological circuits, causing a loop – maybe even a minor seizure in the temporal lobe. You might say, the musical worm has burrowed into your head. How does the earworm make you feel?"

"Feel?"

"I mean, emotionally speaking – what emotions do you associate with it?"

"I don't know – like there's something I need to remember, something I'm missing, or have missed. Something I can't quite reach, that's hidden in those crackly sounds, like a code, or cryptic clue in a crossword. I don't quite know how to put it, Professor: there's some feeling in them I can't put into words."

"Where do you think the answer to the crossword, as it were, might be?"

"Maybe it's at the end of the music. If only I could reach the end, then I might understand. But the end was missing, Professor. And the more the notes and phrases repeat in my head, the more they seem to drain of meaning and emotion. The shorter they become too, so now all I'm hearing are the first few notes: *quavers C, D, E to crotchet*

E, leaning into the tonic, dotted-crotchet F. Does all that make sense?"

"It makes some kind of sense, yes," said the Professor. There was silence for a few seconds – well, silence for him. I could still hear the *Adagietto*, as though on another line.

"Look," he said, finally, "I think the first thing you should try is the psychological route, ERP or even CBT, something like that. Your GP will be able to advise you about these treatments. In your peculiar case, I think the solution might lie within yourself. You might, deep down, hold the key to your own mystery. I would recommend spending time making lists of what the music might represent – thinking hard about what it is you have forgotten or lost. Spend time with yourself. It might be something right under your nose. And yes, maybe you should also try and trace the recording in question. You have a very eccentric earworm, in that the crackles, the specific quality of the recording, seem to be a fundamental part of it. A fascinating and unique case, in my extensive experience. Perhaps you have spent too long with records, not enough time with human beings." He laughed, but it didn't seem to be a joke. "Of course, if the problem persists, tell Sylvie" – I noticed he called her by her first name – "to tell me. There are possible pharmacological treatments, such as clomipramine, for example. But let's not go down that road unless we have to. Let's try other things first."

Over the next few weeks, I tried the other things – well, at least I tried to trace the recording which had caused it all. I listened to Mengelberg's recording of the *Adagietto* from 1926, and Bruno Walter's complete recording of the symphony from 1938; but neither of these was ancient enough, neither had the crackles in the right places, neither could kill off my earworm.

I hunted down every recording ever made of the symphony, new and old. I trawled through catalogues, rang round old contacts, wrote to archivists, recording studios, retired producers. Up till now, I'd been able to find *anything* – if it existed, people said, *The New Yorker* said, the owner of Scores & Shellac could find it. But this time I failed. No-one could help me, and not one of the dozens of recordings I traced came close. None had the *castrati* strings, let alone the wobbles, the hisses and squeaks, which now – in my mind – had infected the music, like a virus. I'd stopped hearing the beauty, the emotion, the melodic line – they'd all drained out of it – and now I just heard noise – the notes and the crackles merged into a meaning-less loop, round and round, round and round – like a worm swallowing its own tail, never stopping, on and on – my whole mind a viral *Adagietto – quavers C, D, E to crotchet E, leaning into tonic F, dotted crotchet* – never stopping, round and round, never stopping, never stopping, never stopping, never . . .

◊

In the end, I decided I had no choice. To be cured, I had to go back to Dr Mahler, in order find out more about the recording, and hopefully get hold of it again.

But there was no answer when I knocked on his door, and the windows were boarded up, the garden overgrown – or doubly overgrown, given that it had already been over-grown in the first place.

I called round for Sylvie. She said no-one knew where he'd gone, or even when he'd gone. The last time anyone had seen him, he'd been sitting on his front lawn, crying to himself. Someone had asked what was wrong, and he'd looked up and said, "It's my Putzi. She's gone. My Almschi. Beethoven. Mozart. They're all gone. I've been waiting all this time."

"He's been away for weeks," said Sylvie, over a bitter instant coffee. "I don't know who boarded up the windows. I did take the key and looked inside, to check he hadn't fallen. But no, no sign at all. It's a mystery. He's a mystery."

"But what about *my* mystery?" I asked. "Where does that leave me? Even your Professor friend thinks I need to find the record again."

"Is that *all* he said?" Sylvie asked. "Do you really think it'll help?"

"Yes – well, maybe. I don't know. He's your friend. Your sister's doctor."

Sylvie nodded, and swirled her coffee round in the mug, staring at it, as though hypnotised: round and round, like an earworm, or a 78.

"Will you stop doing that?" I snapped. Perhaps I shouldn't have, but everything was irritating me.

She looked up at me. For a second, I thought she was going to cry, and I was taken aback, to be honest. It seemed such an over-reaction, not to mention uncharacteristic. Still, I felt I should apologise. "I'm sorry," I said. "You've been very helpful, Sylvie. A good friend. This incessant tune, though – it's driving me mad. Put yourself in my shoes – it's like something's nagging you all the time. Like that feeling you get when you go on a long journey, but know you've left something behind."

"I've never been on a really long trip," said Sylvie, glancing towards the sitting room, from where I could hear her sister moaning ("Help! Help! Sylvie!").

"Oh, I'm sure you have," I said. "Anyway, the point is I've got to find the recording. It's the only answer. The only cure I can think of."

"I wonder," said Sylvie, going back to swirling her coffee. She wasn't much help to me or her sister, that morning.

◊

It wasn't till a couple of mornings later that I realised what she might do for me.

I was on a packed bus to Hanley, the city centre. The earworm seemed louder, faster than before – 80, 82, instead of 78 rpm – and I could hear it above the roar of the engine, the swearing of kids on the back seat, the crying of babies.

Then, out of nowhere, I felt breathing on the back of my neck, and heard someone sitting behind me, someone outside my head, whisper-murmur-grunt the same tune that was inside it: *quavers C, D, E to crotchet E, leaning into tonic F, dotted crotchet*. Someone behind me was echoing my earworm. I froze, chilled into a kind of musical paralysis.

Eventually, the bus stopped, the paralysis passed, and I looked around. Whoever had been whispering to me had got off, washed away with the Hanley shopping crowds.

I followed, and wandered round the shops for hours, as though I were stuck in *Death in Venice* – or, rather, *Death in Hanley* – and I were Gustav von Aschenbach, desperately trying to find someone – someone who was always round the next corner, down the next street. At the time, I assumed that someone was Dr Mahler. Now – well, now I'm not so sure.

Finally, exhausted, footsore, I gave up, and caught the bus back to Hanford. It was early evening by the time I got there.

I knocked on Sylvie's door. She answered, and seemed surprised: "Oh, it's you. Gosh, come in. You look terrible."

"Thanks," I said. We sat together at the kitchen table.

"Sylvie," I said, "I've come to a decision."

She frowned at me from under her dark eyebrows. For the second time, I thought there were tears wobbling in her eyes. I had no idea why. "What?" she asked, very quietly.

"I need to ask you," I said, stammering a little, "I need to ask you – if you don't mind, well, you probably will, but I need to ask you anyway – for the key to Dr Mahler's house."

Sylvie breathed out slowly. "Oh, I see," she said.

"I need that spare key," I explained, "so I can find the record, of course."

"Of course."

Sylvie didn't argue, as I thought she would. She didn't tell me it was illegal, that she'd get thrown off the Neighbourhood Watch committee, that it wasn't fair to put her in this position. Rather, she got up from the table, stepped across the kitchen, and started rooting in one of the drawers.

"Here it is," she said, holding up a key. "Take it. I need it back tonight. Don't let anyone see you." She handed it to me slowly, as if it were heavy, as if it were the key to the underworld, or someone's soul. Under normal circumstances, I'd have laughed, told her it was nothing, not to take her Neighbourhood Watch position so seriously. But something about her manner that evening stopped me. Her behaviour seemed so – I'm not quite sure how to put it – grave, definite, final.

Instead, I just nodded, and was going to say thank you; but she'd already turned away – her sister was calling her from the living room: "Help! I need help, Sylvie! Sylvie!"

I let myself out, and closed the door gently behind me.

◊

Five minutes later, I was turning the key in the front door of 22 Woodside Grove. It opened, and I stepped inside, again closing the door gently behind me.

Because of the boarded-up windows, it should have been pitch black inside. But somehow the dark mountains of rubbish round me seemed to glow, as if they had halos of their own. I pretended the halos weren't there – ignored their warnings – and fumbled for a light switch on either side of the door. I knocked a few things over, and tripped over something with a crash, before I found one. I hoped no-one would see the light outside.

I'd knocked over a Columbia Eclipse. It was on its side, and the tonearm was bent where I'd stepped on it. Normally, I'd be furious at myself for the vandalism – and no doubt the Potteries Official Phonographic Society would have excommunicated me – but this time, I had other things to worry about. I stepped over the Eclipse, to the nearest mountain of 78s.

I started sorting through them, one by one. There were hundreds, perhaps thousands to get through.

At first, I sorted through the record mountain methodically, trying to arrange the 78s I'd examined behind me, in neat towers. Soon, though, the towers tottered, toppled, got mixed up. I tried to clear a bigger space, by piling up other stuff – clothes, books, scores – away from the records. But they toppled too. I stepped over to a second record mountain, started scattering records, even hurling them around.

The *Adagietto* whirling in my head was getting louder, faster, 84, 86, 88 rpm, *Allegretto*, *Allegro pesante*, transformed into a goose-stepping march, *forte*, then *fortissimo*. I couldn't concentrate, the words on the record sleeves were blurring, and I wasn't watching where I was treading. I skidded on a 78 I'd tossed over my shoulder. I fell, and a hundred records and musical scores fell on top of me. I lay there for a moment, covered by 78s, paper and dust, entombed, buried alive in symphonies, overwhelmed by the impossibility of finding a needle in a musical haystack.

I will never find my *Adagietto*, I cried to myself.

I thought of Mahler himself: he could never recapture it, either. He tried to, by quoting it towards the end of his unfinished Tenth Symphony. But it never sounds quite right, quite convincing – as if what it represents is lost – as if it's impossible to return to the love song he wrote years earlier for his wife, Alma – as if the death of their daughter, his disease, and her infidelity have cast a discordant shadow over it – as if the nine-note discord which dominates the first and last movements overshadows everything after and even, retrospectively, everything before it – as if the symphony's terrifying dissonance might bleed out of the score into both past and future . . .

– and I could hear it now, haunting my earworm, quietly disrupting its harmonies, dismembering its musical line . . .

– and cutting through it all, through earworm and discord, I suddenly heard Dr Mahler's voice. I swear I heard it, next to my ear, out of nowhere – whispering, whimpering: "My life has all been paper." I felt his hands on me, smelt something like petrol on his fingers. He seemed to be shaking me. "Where is my Almschi?" he was sobbing. "Tell me, please. I've been waiting for her to come back to me for so long. My Almschi. *Für dich leben! Für dich sterben!*"

I couldn't seem to move, couldn't say anything – I was paralysed, as I had been on the bus. All I remember thinking is: how remarkable, how strange, how terrible love must be, to make you wait for years, or even decades for someone who never turns up.

Then I heard a shrill trumpet shrieking A above everything, like an annunciation from the unconscious, and the nine-note dissonance crashed around me once more, blotting out the *Adagietto*, blotting out Dr Mahler's voice, blotting out everything but the smell of petrol.

◊

When I came to, in the hospital, after the most severe seizure I'd had in years, everything inside me seemed quiet. The *Adagietto* had finally gone and so too had the discord.

At first, I felt an intense emptiness, almost as if I wanted the earworm back. Soon enough, though, the emptiness was filled by pain, by the soreness of my legs and bandaged hands, where I'd suffered burns from the fire. The fire had been put out fairly quickly, I was told: it had destroyed most of the house's contents – including the records and antique collection of gramophones – but the house itself remained intact, and Dr Mahler was fine. He'd been sectioned, of course, but was otherwise unharmed.

The police came to question me, and the Chairman of the Potteries Official Phonographic Society sent a card. No-one else visited or sent messages. I waited in that hospital bed for what felt like years, decades, though really it was only a few days. But no. No-one else came to see me.

No-one.

My life, I realised, had all been paper, shellac.

J. S. Bach, Double Concerto for Two Violins, Performed by Alma and Arnold Rosé

Based on a true story

And when she puts on the long-lost 78s, and the needle discovers the music through a forest of crackles, Rosa visibly jumps

— a jolt of recognition not merely for the music itself (which she knows, used to play herself), but for one of the performers, Alma Rosé, with her unmistakable tone, technique, phrasing, *vibrato*

— all of which, despite her more-recent nerve deafness, tinnitus and, above all, musicophobia, Rosa remembers, could never forget, from long, long ago

— a terrible long-long-ago she doesn't want to remember, but which the music, and the second violinist are remembering for her . . .

◊

Largo ma tanto, 12 / 8, F major, *sicilienne* rhythm, regular as barbed wire, with no up-beat, no Quarantine Block, just straight into

exposition: subject theme on second violin, played by Alma, lightly accompanied by the orchestra – all heard-re-membered by Rosa as it was years after the recording, in the Birch Grove, Alma standing tall, dark-haired, very thin, the inscrutable supervisor, *kapo*, number 50381, accompanied by a *Lagerkapelle* made up not just of violins, violas, 'cellos and harpsichord, but also mandolins, accordion, flute, guitar, anything they could find in the camp, anyone they could save, as well as the tramp-tramp-tramp of the *Kommando*s, the recorded orchestra infected with the dark future as surely as if gas and smoke might travel back in time,

the orchestra now *poco piano*, drilled by the formidable Alma back into line, F, descending through quavers E and D to dominant C, descending through quavers B-flat-A-G-E-F, heavy on the *portamento*, up to B-flat, then quavers A, C, F followed by semi-quaver run G-F-E-D all leading up to

entry of first violin – on this recording father Arnold's answer to daughter's song, and, later, in the camp, Rosa's own trembling answer to 50381's song – on dominant C above the stave, dotted crotchet tied to quaver hanging like purple-black smoke in the air, transposing the world up a fifth, into C major, descending to new dominant, G, and all the while the second violin is accompanying with counter-subject, incessant semi-quavers, rising in sequence from E to F to G to A,

like rising (*"Aufstehen!"*) before the frozen sunrises of

'43, from the three-tiered *cojas* into a grey room, pulling on her blue skirt, woollen stockings, striped jacket and white head scarf, swallowing metallic soup, then *Vorwärts Marsch!* in rows of five from Block 12, past the electro-cuted *Stoffpuppen* hanging off the fences, three hundred or so yards to the rotting platform, outside the gates, and then the music – *Arbeitsmarsch* after *Arbeitsmarsch* for the hundreds, thousands, shuffle-marching past the orchestra to work – shivering out of her violin, diffusing, radiating, echoing,

echoing back to the barracks, where she is locked up again for twelve or fourteen hours of echoing rehearsal a day, sometimes longer, as though her *kapo* is terrified of what might happen if the musical echoes stop, the sounds and sights which might no longer be drowned out from beyond the barracks,

so the echoes don't stop, the two solo violins continue calling to each other, as if across a huge distance, across time, or through those longed-for Red Cross telegrams from loved ones far away,

until STOP

and the closeness disintegrates, the two are separated, the line goes dead, the telegrams dry up,

and the violins take turns to murmur semi-quaver fare-wells, ever-quieter, as if unheard by the other, in C minor,

a key which slides down into A major, pulled down, down,

into that drowning clay mud, which seemed then to have taken over the world, sucking down still-twitching corpses, *Muselmänner*, trees, sky, memories, colour, bird song and melody, to a place where, for Rosa at least, major keys sound dissonant, where common chords shock the ear as much as the twitching dead on the *Leichenwagen* horrify inadvertently raised eyes

— major keys and common chords like F major, which the music has finally attained again, with the recapitulation of the main subject, apparently untouched, stoical, hard-edged, always lowering gazes to the ground, never looking up into an officer's eyes, never looking beyond the nearest wall, never peering round corners or into distances, even middle distances, where five belching chimneys, rifle fire, dogs, Block 25, *Experimenteller Block*, the *Revier*, the *Leichenwagen*, the *Selektionen*, and the pesticide Zyklon-B all happen,

a musical myopia, a terminal *Blocksperre*, confining Rosa's hearing, Rosa's vision to the notes on the musical stand in front, to the strict rhythm, crotchet-quaver-crotchet-quaver, to these bar-lines,

after another two of which there comes that long-held C above the stave which, again, seems untouched by what is happening around it, what has happened, but isn't really, because a recapitulation is always overshadowed by what has gone before, even or especially when it pretends not to be,

and finally, finally, the coda is ushered in *piano* by a high C on the first violin, followed by the semi-quavers of the counter-subject, somehow half-hearted, bidding *Abschied* to the second violin, which limps through the episodic material

into the final triplets, *forte*, heavy *ritenuto*, the perfect cadence on a final F-major chord almost perfunctory, as though this music, with its seemingly infinite runs of semi-quavers, wouldn't find an ending if someone didn't just draw a line somewhere and say, "That's it, I've had enough, *das Ende*"

as they did with Alma in April '44,

though for the violinist who survived, for Rosa herself, the F-major end did not come; and long after her duets with Alma had apparently stopped, long after the latter's poisoning, long after the camp had been disbanded, for months, years and decades afterwards, Rosa might still have this music's incessant semi-quavers running through her head, taking them to and from another camp, and then across a continent to a lost father's house in Great Britain, and eventually to a small provincial city in the Midlands, the notes still echoing round and round in Rosa's mind, trapped like a *Häftling* in a never-ending camp, laboriously semi-quavering for survival, not joy, with no respite, no let-up, a mental *Arbeit macht* certainly not *frei*, the semi-quavers never reaching the silence at the end of those un-applauded Sunday concerts in the Sauna, in front of the seated officers, the *Lagerführerinnen*, the *Kapo*s, *Blockowa*s, the shaved hordes ordered to watch and listen to Bach, hollow-eyed, hollow-eared from doorways,

and long after those hordes have been hollowed out further by memory, the Bachian semi-quavers mingle strangely, enigmatically with spectral counterpoints only Rosa can hear from the distant Sunday concerts, from the dismal work-marches, from Beethoven's Fifth, *The Blue Danube*, orchestrations of Schubert's piano music, arrangements of arias by Verdi, and – although the orchestra's music was meant to be purified, *judenrein* – even *Entartete Musik*, tip-toeing in under the noses of the officers, while no *Lagerführerin* was paying attention: Dvořák's *Slavonic Dances*, Mendelssohn's Violin Concerto, Mahler's *Adagietto*,

and hearing-remembering this Mendelssohn-Mahler-Dvořák-Verdi-Schubert-Strauss-Beethoven-Bach aural palimpsest now, on these old 78s, in her own head, Rosa tries not to cry with the realisation that the weaving semi-quavers aren't all barbed wire, electrical fences, cinders, ovens and searchlights

– that they aren't all glares and threats from Alma, that conductor-violinist of whom she'd been so afraid, but closed-eye nods as well, a final *ppp* "*schön*"

– that perhaps what she'd thought of as fear for the *kapo* is also a kind of love

– that the common chords, the F majors on the records aren't all dissonance or machine-gun fire, or at least not any longer

– that, after all these years of dissonant semi-quavering terror in her head, of trauma-induced *amusica*, it's not the semi-quavers she should fear, but the un-applauded silence which comes at the end of those semi-quavers:

"*Ruhe! Ruhe!*" someone is calling in her past.

"*Frieden!*"

"He never writes to me no more"

A story for children

"HE NEVER WRITES to me no more," she says.

"How can he write to you when he's been dead for fifty years?" I say.

Then she cries a bit.

After a while, she brightens up, and says:

"He never writes to me no more."

And I say:

"How can he write to you when he's been dead for fifty years?"

And she cries again.

"Grandma," I say, "Korea was a long time ago. Grandpa was a long time ago. It's 2004, Grandma. We've got iPods. And texting, so you don't need letters."

"Oh," she says, and she's quiet for a bit. The clock tick-tock-ticks in the corner and I think about the door and tonight's telly. To be honest, this place frightens me. It smells of old wee. Down the corridor, someone else's grandma is screaming that goblins are using her toothbrush.

"He never writes to me no more."

"Grandma," I sigh.

My mum says that Grandma's got a disease called Alzheimer's which makes her forget. She says it gives her a kind of amnesia, if you know what that is. She says she can't cope with it any more, cos Grandma keeps forgetting that Grandpa's long dead. We have to keep reminding her. And it's news all over again. And she cries for him. And forgets again. And wonders where he is.

It's like Grandpa's dying over and over in her head, every few minutes.

But really he died millions of years ago. There was a war in a country called Korea. He was on America's side. He died when they were attacked at Yalu River on the 25th October, 1950. I know all about it, you see. I looked it up. Grandpa died of drowning, they reckoned, and they didn't find his body. One day, his letters to Grandma just stopped.

"He never writes to me no more."

Grandma says this and cries, and for the billionth time shows me the bundle of brown letters she keeps in a biscuit tin in the corner. Funny, but she never forgets where that is. Personally, I'd prefer it if the letters were biscuits. That's what normal grandmas would give me. Normal grandmas'd pat me on the head, say "Ooh, you've grown," and give me grandma-type biscuits, like Rich Tea or Digestives. And perhaps a few quid. But no, not my Alzheimer's grandma. I just get smelly old letters.

The letters are the letters Grandpa sent her from Korea. The last one, on top, is from the 24th October, 1950. He must've been already dead when she got it – kinda spooky, I reckon. It's very short, and he says: 'Dear Glad, thanks

for your letter. Tomorrow's a biggish day. Will write when
it's over. Mosquitoes nasty as ever.' Then there's some blah-
blah-lovey-dovey stuff, and he signs off once and (I suppose)
for ever: 'Love, Frank.'

"He never writes to me no more."

Mum lost it yesterday when Grandma said that for
the trillionth time. She burst into tears and said she hated
seeing her mum like this. Then she shouted at Grandma:
"He's dead, don't you get it? Dead dead dead dead dead." I
thought the word sounded weird, repeated like that. It goes
sort of funny, as if you're not sure what it means any more.
But no-one else was laughing. Everyone else was shouting
and crying at once. Even the hard nurse with the tattoo.
And Grandma was in floods cos Grandpa had died again.

I didn't know what to do. It was horrid.

So – and I know you'll think it's really weird what I'm
going to tell you. But anyway, let's get it over with, and you
can think whatever you like. Who cares.

You see, last night, I sat down and wrote a letter. Never
written one before except at school. And not even at school
a love letter. They don't teach you that in Year 5.

I'd nicked one of the old letters from the biscuit tin, and
I did my best to copy Grandpa's ancient style of writing –
squiggly 'Ts' and spidery bits. It was dead hard and took
ages, I tell you. Then I folded it in an envelope, got a stamp
from my mum's purse, and addressed it to Grandma in the
home. I didn't write 'Grandma' on it – I put 'Mrs Gladys
Hallwood' plus the home's address. Then I shoved it in the
pillar box down the street.

Feel free to think I'm weird when you find out what it
was about. Maybe I am. All I know is that when I went

today Grandma had stopped saying "He never writes to me no more." Instead, she was smiling in a long-time-ago way, if you know what I mean. She even offered me a Rich Tea. Though still no cash.

Anyway, here goes. What I wrote went like this:

Dear Glad,

Hello from Korea. I'm sorry I haven't written you for the last fifty-five years, but I've been a bit caught up with some stuff. You know what wars are like. So sorry about that.

But here I am again. Things are cool in Seoul. Wish you were here.

I just wanted to say that I miss you truck-loads. You're great and we'll see each other again very soon.

With love and all that, Frank.

Changelessness

At 3 A.M., unable to sleep, she creeps downstairs. The living room is exactly as she left it: the empty wine glass on the coffee table, the TV on standby, the marking scattered by the rocking chair, the row of teddies gazing at her, glassily. Nothing is different. Nothing has changed in three hours of wide-eyed insomnia – not unlike the teddies – of ceiling-staring, of a kind of unsleeping paralysis.

Still, there's something about that nothing – something about the changelessness – which makes the hairs rise on the back of her neck, makes her sob: *ohmygodohmygodohmygod, it's all the same. It's all just as I left it.* The wine glass hasn't refilled itself; the TV hasn't turned itself on, isn't broadcasting white noise from which emerges a disembodied bass growl, mumbling: *Gone, they're gone, gone, they're gone, gone*, over and over; the marking on the floor hasn't been tidied up; the teddies haven't blinked.

She stares straight at them. They still don't blink.

She holds their gaze. They still don't blink.

She blinks first.

And then sinks to her knees, tidying the marking into a neat pile – as *he* would have done – and shaking the teddies, trying to animate them, throwing them about the room – as *they* would have done.

But none of it is convincing – neither the grown-up tidiness, nor the childhood mess, neither the neat essays, nor the scattered teddies – because *she* has done these things. They feel like half-hearted imitations of *real* tidiness, *real* mess, because they didn't happen without her, when she wasn't in the room – which is what she wants more than anything in the world.

More than anything in the world, she wants to come downstairs to find the room rearranged, different, so she can be irritated at someone: *Why did you do that?*

She's crying now, lying on the floor in the foetal position, hugging one of the teddies, speaking for the TV in a strange voice that isn't her own: *They're gone, gone, they're gone, gone. I let them go, and they aren't coming back.*

"*Tell me what you know*"

"I DON'T KNOW anything."

"Tell me how you *feel* then."

"Honestly, I don't feel anything. Please. Please don't. Fucking hell. Please don't do *that*."

But she does anyway, slicing lengthwise down her forearm, a bit deeper this time.

"Please," she cries. Tears squeeze themselves from her eyes and blood from the cut. "Please stop."

"I thought you said you don't feel anything."

"I don't," she says, "but please stop. That's enough, surely?"

"No it's not. It's not enough, and I won't stop. Not until you have told me. Told me everything. Told me what you're feeling about *him*. There's something, like, wrong about it – something wrong about how you feel, and you're going to tell me what it is. You know what it is. Deep down, you *know*."

"There's nothing. Honestly. I don't know anything. I don't feel anything. I never feel anything."

She is holding the arm over the sink. It doesn't bleed as much as she'd thought, or perhaps hoped, but a few drops splash into the bowl. She counts them: seven. One for each year in care.

"One last time: tell me. Tell me, for fuck's sake, tell me."

"No. I can't. I won't."

She screws up her eyes tight, placing one of the scissor blades against the skin again.

"I won't. I won't tell you. I won't."

"You don't owe *him* anything, you know. *He's* the one who abandoned *you.* You don't owe him any loyalty. You can tell me the truth. You owe *me*, not him. *I'm* the important one here. For fuck's sake – he sods off when you need him most, you don't see him for years, then you see him once, and suddenly you won't even, like, talk to me. Have you got no fucking memory? The cunt left you in this fucking hell-hole. He left you. And you see him once for, like, half an hour, and you forget about everything – and somehow think you owe him your loyalty, silence, or some shit. Well, let me remind you: you don't owe him anything. He's shit, he's nothing – let alone a *father*. He's not a *real* father. He was a stupid sperm in a car crash with an egg seventeen years ago. He's nothing more than a walking sperm dispenser."

There's a pause after the rant, as she tries to control her breathing: in-out-in-out. Then she speaks more quietly, gently: "Please, you can tell me. I won't be angry. I promise. Just tell me how you feel. I know something's going on. I know there's something wrong. It's obvious."

"There's nothing to tell you. Honestly. I don't feel anything."

"Then you've left me no choice, you stupid bitch." She presses the blade through the skin, deeper this time – as if it were possible to cut down to the unconscious, to find what's down there, buried under skin, flesh, bones, to prise it out. She stifles her own cry, and draws the scissors down the forearm again, cutting a parallel line of blood with the other two. This time, the blood flows freely from the wound.

"Tell me," she demands, one last time.

"I'll never tell you. Never." She is sobbing now, and tears and blood mix in the sink. "Fuck you," she says, exhilarated, intoxicated by pain. "I'll never tell you. Nevernevernevernevernevernevernevernevernevernevernevernevernevernevernevernevernevernevernevernevernevernevernevernevernevernevernevernevernevernevernevernevernevernevernevernevernevernevernevernevernevernevernevernevernevernevernevernevernevernevernevernevernevernevernevernevernevernevernevernevernevernevernevernevernevernevernevernever."

But the blood and tears are betraying her to herself, coalescing in the sink like a confession, a denunciation: *she loves him*, they are whispering, *the stupid bitch still loves him.*

High Dependency

THEN WE WENT to the hospital.
Then we came home.
Then we went to the hospital.
Then we came home.
Then we went to the hospital.
Our twins slept. A passing consultant mumbled something about vital signs, ups and downs. Machines bleeped, as if swearing to themselves.
Then we went home.
Then we went to the hospital.
Then we came home.
We ate a lukewarm takeaway. We ignored the phone. It kept ringing, ringing. We picked up the phone, and said: "Yes, yes, no, no, still no change." We went to bed.
We went to the hospital. In our dreams.
We came home. In our dreams.
We woke up and went to the hospital in reality.
A couple of people visited. We got their faces and names mixed up with other faces and names.
We came home. We watched *World's Worst Serial Killers* on TV till three.

We snored on the sofa.

We woke up, had four hours in bed, then went to the hospital.

Our twins cried, slept, pooed, slept, cried, pooed.

Another parent muttered something about a case of meningitis on the ward. Then said we should always look on the bright side and pray – though whether to Jesus or Monty Python, she didn't specify.

In the afternoon, the neonatal nurses dimmed the lights and played Mozart's *Eine Kleine Nachtmusik* to rows of premature babies.

We went home. A lightbulb in the hallway had blown, so we had to change it. It blew again. The microwave burnt our tea. We tried to wash up, but the hot water was off. We turned the boiler off and on again. It still didn't work. We rang a plumber, but couldn't find a time when he could come and fix it and we'd be in. We rang another plumber. And another. We cried. We went to bed.

Next morning, we went to the hospital. Without a shower.

A passing consultant flicked through the twins' notes, mumbled something about vital signs, downs and ups. Machines bleeped, as if swearing to themselves.

We sat in the cafeteria for breakfast, slurping lukewarm soup. One of us went to express. The other stayed sitting for a while.

When we both got back to the ward, they'd dimmed the lights, and were playing the prems *Eine Kleine Nachtmusik* again, orchestrated for strings and machinic bleeps.

We reached through holes in an incubator, touched a hand the size and texture of a petal.

One day, we whispered, one day, in years to come, we will play you *Eine Kleine Nachtmusik* and it will trigger in you something distant, something infinitesimal, like an infection, like cells dividing, like the tiny zigzags on a monitor, the bleep-bleep-bleeps which will never stop. Must never stop. The four of us, we will not be stuck in this twilight world forever. There will be a future, not just an ever-recurring present, believe me – a future, years away, when we are not here, trapped in this enchanted circle. Then you will hear Mozart's little night music, and it will remind you of something you can't recall, something beyond memory's horizon – it will teleport your unconscious back here, for a fleeting moment. A bleep, no more, and then gone.

The petal closed.

We went home.

Scablands

I.

"I'LL CANE YOU, boy."

The voice – baritone, resonant, strangely sorrowful – comes from the school library. The word "boy" is elongated, with a slight flourish upwards, like a verbal serif: "I'll cane you, *boooooooyyy*."

The new first-year boy hurries past the library door, trembling, near tears: what kind of place is this, where even libraries threaten you with the cane?

"I'll cane you, boy" follows him down the corridor.

At the end of the corridor there is a prefect, who snarls at him that he's gone the wrong way round the one-way system, "Go back. Outside. Otherwise . . ."

The boy goes back, hurrying past the library door again: "I'll cane you, boy!"

Eventually, he finds a door and bursts into daylight. He breathes in deeply, and looks up: the playground, a lunchtime battlefield, stretches out before him.

2.

"I heard your dad was a scab," hisses a fifth-year girl, "a scab from *Scabland* – Derby or Nottingham, somewhere shit like that." She shoves the new boy backwards. He crashes into a fifth-year boy, who seems very, very tall when he turns round to see what's going on.

"Oi, what d'you think you're doing?"

"He's a fucking scab, Terry," says the girl. Two of the older boy's friends also turn round at the word. They're both wearing frayed NCB donkey jackets.

"Who's a scab?"

"He is. Well, his dad was. Is."

"Is that true?" ask the fifth-year boys, closing in.

"No."

The girl closes in too. "You calling me a liar?"

"No. Please. I mean . . ."

"What? Go on then: what *do* you mean?" she says, shoving the new boy again. He stares upwards – the sky above him is all angry faces.

"I mean, didn't that finish two years ago? And my dad . . ."

"It's not finished. Never will be. Once a scab always a scab." She sneers at the boys, "Just listen to him. You can hear it in his accent. So fucking posh. Scab's voice."

"Oh come on, what's his voice got to do with it, Kez? You and your old man think everyone's a scab, or a faggot."

"His voice's got everything to do with it, Terry." She stamps down hard on the new boy's foot. He yelps. "He's not from round here. He's come over from *Scabland* – y'know, UDM country."

"But my dad wasn't a scab. He couldn't have been."

"Why not?"

"Because he wasn't a miner."

She frowns. "Wasn't a miner? What was he, then? Management? Pig?"

"He was a teacher."

"And what's he now then?"

"Nothing."

"Nothing?"

"He's dead. He died." The new boy speaks breathlessly, not wanting to be stopped till he's finished the story. "It was a few months ago. We didn't live here then. We lived near Derby. He had a heart attack. That's why me and my mum came here. To stay with grandpa. That's why I've come to this school now, in June." He slows, out of breath, and adds quietly, "That's why: because my dad died."

The fifth-year boys glance at one another, back off slightly – as if he might be infected by something. "Okay, well then . . ."

The girl, though, isn't about to give in – isn't about to lose Terry's attention now she has it. "He fucking deserved it. Fucking deserved to die. *Scab*."

"Hey, Kez, bit harsh. P'raps we ought to let . . ."

"Nah. His dad was a scab. We can't leave it."

"But my dad wasn't a scab," says the new boy, desperate. "He wasn't. Honest. I told you. He was a teacher."

She spits on the new boy's blazer at the word "teacher." "A bloody teacher – that's as bad as a scab. All of them're against us. Scabs. Tories. The lot of them."

"I don't think my dad was Conservative. He said he voted SDP or something."

"It's all the same. Tory scum. *Scab*."

She pushes the new boy into Terry. Terry pushes him back.

"Come on, Kez. Leave him. He's not worth it."

The girl can't leave it now she's got this far. She pushes the new boy into one of the other fifth-year boys. They all start shoving him – the boys half-heartedly, Kez much harder. "My dad would've beaten the shit out of yours. Alive or dead," says Kez.

She shoves the new boy so hard that he stumbles and trips in Terry's direction. Terry backs up, lets him fall to the ground, head-first.

The new boy is crying. One arm of his glasses is bent and he has a graze on the side of his head. Kez takes a step towards him, ready to stamp on him. Terry blocks her way, holds her arm. "Let him go, Kez, for fuck's sake. He's not worth it. And look –"

Terry tilts his head to the left, and Kez glances in the direction he's indicating. Across the playground, above the heads of the children, the deputy's reptilian stare is slowly turning towards them.

While Kez is distracted, the new boy gets up, tries to put his glasses on straight – and runs.

3.

The new boy is back in the corridor, panting, leaning against the closed door. He touches his forehead. There's a bit of blood on his fingertips. His head is stinging.

He looks up. The prefect from earlier has disappeared. The corridor is deserted, dark, quiet.

The new boy tiptoes down it, hoping he might get away with passing the library unheard.

"I'll cane you boy." The voice seems louder this time.

The new boy starts running, round the corner, straight into the prefect and Kez. How she got here so quickly, he has no idea. It's almost spooky, he thinks, like a lot of things in this strange school.

"You again!" growls Kez, pushing him away.

"You've been told before," says the prefect, who's obviously one of Kez's mates.

The new boy backs away, then turns and dashes round the corner, along the corridor again. He can hear footsteps coming after him.

He doesn't know where to go: behind him are Kez and the prefect; outside, in the playground, are the fifth-form boys. He stops, trapped.

Kez and the prefect are right behind him.

He darts through the door to his right, into the library.

"I'll cane you, boy."

Kez and the prefect skid to a halt in the doorway.

"I'll cane you all."

They glare at the new boy, as he backs away from them, into the library. They don't cross the threshold — as though it's enchanted, as though there's some invisible barrier between the library and the outside world. The boy wonders what fresh hell he's stepped into.

He bumps into something soft and swivels round to see what it is: a tatty armchair. A tall, painfully thin man is slumped in the chair, wearing a beige suit and waistcoat, his fly-away hair wavering indecisively between blond and white.

The man in beige splutters something – somehow he's managed to doze off in the few seconds since declaiming "I'll cane you all" – and half rises to his feet. His left hand reaches for a cane propped next to his chair.

"What on earth are you doing in here, boy? I'll cane you for this."

The new boy now backs away from him, and then stops, realising he's in another trap, stuck this time between a cane on the one hand, and Kez and the prefect on the other. There seems to be nowhere in this school which isn't a trap, where he can be safe. He wants to go home. And even there are tears, shouts, his grandpa's belt.

"Sorry, sir, I . . ."

"And what are you two staring at?" the man in beige declares towards the doorway, brandishing his cane at Kez and the prefect. "Get away from there, or I'll cane you too." He steps over to the door and slams it in their faces.

He turns on the new boy, tapping the cane against his other hand, testing it out, rehearsing for a beating. He advances, and the boy shrinks into his over-sized uniform.

"Please, sir, I . . . Please . . ."

The man in beige glowers over the new boy, testing the cane on his own right palm with increasing force – almost as if he wants to hurt himself.

"Please, sir, I was only . . ."

The man glances down at his palm. "My skin's so tough these days. Can't seem to get through to it, however much I try. Your skin, though, is nice and young and tender. It'll hurt a lot. Well it *would* do if . . ."

The new boy is trembling, wishing he were back in

the playground. At least he understands the kids there. He lets out a sob.

In response, the man's shoulders droop – he seems to lose height in front of the boy's eyes.

"Oh, for goodness sake, less of that." The man props the cane against the side of the armchair, reaches into his breast pocket and takes out a handkerchief the size of the boy's head. "That's quite enough. Blow your nose, boy." The boy does as he's told, and hands back the handkerchief. The man takes it, folds it neatly, and puts it away. Then he steps over to his armchair and slumps into it. "Ah," he says, "that's better. Enough excitement for one lunchtime."

The boy is still sniffing. "I thought you were going to cane me, sir."

"Oh, do be quiet," the man says. "Stop snivelling. Empty threat and all that." He's staring at a television in the corner opposite, sandwiched between library shelves. A test match is on. The volume is down low: all the boy can hear is a hum, the odd crack of ball on bat, funereal commentary. The man in beige seems hypnotised by the TV: his eyes move, indeed, his whole head moves, almost imperceptibly, with the ball, following it each time it's bowled, each time it's shot across the field.

"I don't understand, sir," he says, looking from screen to man and back again.

"Empty threat, boy," says the man, still staring at the screen. "Like most things in life."

"What's an empty threat?"

"That," says the man, nodding his head to one side, in the vague direction of the cane. "I might threaten you with it – after a whole lifetime of doing so, I can't seem to stop – but technically I am no longer permitted to use it. I'm told it's now against your human rights, boy, against the law. The Law is an ass, of course. But my opinion and experience notwithstanding, the trusty cane, the teacher's long-time friend and ally, is obsolete, out of time – a bit like oneself."

"Oh," says the boy, nodding slowly. In theory, he is aware that corporal punishment has been banned; in practice, though, he cannot quite believe it – and the ghost of violence seems to haunt the whole school, top to bottom. There are threats, empty or otherwise, everywhere.

"Empty threats, you know, can be most effective. For instance, they keep people out of here." For a moment, the man turns to the boy, an eyebrow raised. "By and large, that is." The man's gaze returns to the test match.

The boy shifts his weight from one leg to the other. He would leave of his own accord – he knows he isn't really welcome – except for the thought of what's outside, beyond the enchanted library. He suspects the man will tell him to go any minute, anyway; and he half-expects that Kez and the prefect will still be standing outside the library door when he opens it.

Instead, the man sighs. "Ah, the good old days, boy. The cane. Discipline. Culture. What have we done?" His voice quietens, deepens, "'Jesu, Jesu, the mad days that I have spent! And to see how many of my old acquaintances are dead.'"

"What's that, sir? I don't understand, sir."

"I'm sure you don't, boy. No-one does any longer. People keep telling me they don't understand me – that the pupils don't understand me. At some point, I seem to have lost the ability to communicate with a younger generation, to work out what is an appropriate register for youthful ears. Or perhaps I never had it. It was hardly a priority years ago. During my own school years, I don't recall any of our masters adapting their diction or syntax to suit different age groups. Communication has become so difficult, so stratified, don't you think?"

The boy shakes his head and nods at the same time.

"Well, never mind." The man looks up again at the boy, then leans over to his right, and draws a plastic chair over, next to his. He pats it. "To return to your question, boy. It was a quotation from some long-forgotten playwright called William Shakespeare. You may have heard of him, you may not. One cannot be certain these days. Anyway, while you are here, you might as well sit down and watch some of this godforsaken test match with me. England, naturally, is losing to one of her ex-colonies."

The boy sits down next to the man in beige. The man reaches over – without taking his eyes off the screen – and offers the boy a long, bony finger. The boy looks down at it and decides he's meant to shake it. "Pleased to meet you," says the man. "I am Mr Chandler. And you?"

The new boy hesitates.

"Come on, spit it out," says Mr Chandler. "You must know who you are."

"It's not that, sir," says the boy. "It's just . . ." It's just that the question is unexpected: this is the first time since the boy arrived at the school that anyone has asked him his name.

4.

At half past three, Kez and Terry are standing outside the school gates, as crowds of kids – most of whom are smaller than them – swarm past. Terry is about to light Kez's cigarette, when the latter suddenly lunges away and fishes the new boy out of the crowd, by the collar.

"Trying to sneak past us, *scab?*" she asks, shaking him.

Terry yawns. "Oh, come on, Kez. Let's have a smoke in peace."

"I can't. He's a scab. My dad won't ever leave scabs alone, won't ever forget what they did. That's what he says."

Kez shakes the new boy. She's strong – the boy isn't sure his feet are touching the ground. It's hard to breathe.

"Please, let me down."

She shakes him a bit more, then lets go of his collar. He drops down, gasping for breath; but before he can escape, she grabs him by the ear instead – in the same way she's seen teachers grab pupils, when it was allowed. In the same way her dad grabbed her a few weeks ago, before he crushed her head against the kitchen wall.

The new boy squirms, tears rising to his eyes. "Please . . ."

"Kez, come on," says Terry, exhaling smoke into the new boy's face, "for fuck's sake."

"No, I won't *come on*. Look at him. Bloody worm." She squeezes, twists the new boy's ear harder. He cries out. A few kids surging past peer over to see what's happening. None intervene.

"You got away from us at lunch, didn't you – probably reckoned you'd get away now, too." She holds him down by the ear, almost twisting him into the ground – and speaks over his head at Terry, "You know where the runt escaped to? The library. He hid in there with Chandler. Chandler, for fuck's sake." She laughs, like it's a joke. Terry doesn't join in, so she speaks directly to the new boy again, "Did you enjoy being in there with Chandler, scab? Two scabs together. Yeah, we all know what he thinks – he's a fucking Tory scab too." She speaks through her teeth, "Did he use the cane on you? Did he take down your trousers and beat the shit out of you? Did you enjoy it? You and Chandler are the same. Gay Tory scabs. Everyone knows about him. Everyone knows why he's shut in the library. Can't help himself touching boys, dirty bastard. And you're the same. Fucking queers."

The new boy is crying now, tears dropping onto the pavement. She's still twisting his ear with one hand and is pulling his tie back with the other. He's choking.

"Kez, leave him," says Terry, taking one last drag of the cigarette and stubbing it out on the wall next to him.

Kez pulls the tie harder. Her face is screwed up in anger. Terry looks at it. It reminds him of her father, who called him a "fucking queer" last time he went round. He decides he doesn't fancy Kez after all, never really has.

"I said *stop it*." He grabs Kez's wrist, wrenching it away from the new boy's tie. She yells in pain and lets go of the ear as well. Terry pushes her hard – much harder than he'd intended – and she tumbles backwards. The crowd parts, and she lands on her backside. One or two kids stop and point, giggling.

"That's enough," says Terry. He stares down at her for a moment, thinking he's about to say sorry for hurting her, for pushing too hard. In the end, he doesn't bother, turns and stalks off.

The new boy doesn't see any of this, because he's already legged it in the other direction.

5.

Next day, the new boy hides in the library again. He can't think of anywhere else to go, and – after an initial "I'll cane you, boy" – Mr Chandler doesn't seem to mind. He makes the boy a cup of tea and they sit watching the test match together. One of the English batsmen is bowled out.

"Out again," says Mr Chandler. "What a shower this dear old England of ours has become."

"Mr Chandler, sir," says the boy, who's been shuffling awkwardly on the chair, mulling over some of the things Kez said yesterday. "Please can I ask you a question?"

"You may indeed, if it helps you stop that damned wriggling," says Mr Chandler. "You may ask me any question, as long as it is not 'To be or not to be.' That one I cannot, in all honesty, answer."

"I don't think that's the question I want to ask," says the boy.

"Go on then, out with it."

"I was wondering why you're always in here, sir," says the boy. He knows – without quite understanding why – this is a big question to ask, and that it might hurt Mr Chandler's feelings. But he needs to ask it, because he's obscurely worried by Kez's accusations, both about Mr Chandler and himself.

"I am not *always* in here, boy," says Mr Chandler. "I do not spend the nights here, and I do sally forth on occasion to teach." His tone quietens, and he frowns a little. "Though admittedly, in that latter capacity, I am now restricted to teaching proletarian dullards how to spell their names, rather than leading intelligent pupils such as yourself through the grand corridors of Western culture. In that sense, yes, I am certainly confined, pedagogically speaking, to a small space, a room no bigger than this, as it were."

The new boy doesn't follow everything Mr Chandler says but knows that his question has not yet been answered. It makes him even more uncomfortable.

"Why are you still shuffling, boy?" asks Mr Chandler, after a few seconds' silence.

"I know you're not here *all* the time," says the boy – although he didn't know, hadn't thought about it, "but why are you in here most of the school day, sir?" The boy takes a big bite of his tongue sandwich and waits for the answer.

"Because, to be frank," says Mr Chandler – and the boy wonders what's coming, "to speak to you man to man, or rather man to boy, I am in the process of being rendered obsolete."

"I don't understand, sir."

"That is to say, I am yesterday's man, a relic of a bygone era, consigned to a state of semi-exile. Like Dante's Virgil, I am banished to this armchair limbo, somewhere between employment and retirement." The boy jumps, as, all of a sudden, Mr Chandler stands, towers above him, declaiming:

I am thy father's spirit,
Doom'd for a certain term to walk the night,
And for the day confined to fast in fires,
Till the foul crimes done in my days of nature
Are burnt and purged away.

Seemingly exhausted by the effort, Mr Chandler sinks back into the armchair, breathing heavily. "Enough exercise for today," he says, picking up his cup and saucer, sipping his tea.

"In short," continues Mr Chandler, in a voice which reminds the boy of sunsets, "the powers that be will not grant me early retirement, but simultaneously abhor my teaching methods. Hence, I am to spend the twilight years of my so-called 'career' ensconced in this armchair, over-seeing an under-used library, with occasional sallies to lead imbeciles towards the Holy Grail of a grade 4 CSE – or whatever they call these things nowadays.

"Some teaching careers end on a high with a grand leaving-do, slaps on the back, a carriage clock. They are the comedies. Some careers end on a low, with nervous break-downs, suicides. They are the tragedies. Then there are the careers, like my own, which merely fade away. There's no term for those careers, no genre. They defy literature: they are neither comedy nor tragedy, neither *Goodbye Mr Chips*, nor *The Browning Version*."

"Oh," says the boy.

There's something in that "Oh," which makes Mr Chandler angry – which causes him to slam down his cup and saucer on the low table in front of him. The boy jumps for a second time.

"I'm sorry, sir, I didn't mean . . ."

"Of course I know what everyone says about me behind my back," sputters Mr Chandler, sending spittle flying in all directions. "Of course I am not unaware of the vile rumours that circulate this godforsaken dungeon – rumours which persist even when everyone knows they are malicious and entirely false." He hits the arm of his chair, and the broken blood vessels on his face turn pink, then red.

The boy tries to reassure him. "Please, sir. I didn't mean to upset you. I've not heard any rumours." He swallows, quickly moving on from the lie. "Please, sir, don't think about it. Have a Custard Cream."

Mr Chandler glances down at the biscuit barrel, which the boy has opened and is offering to him. His shoulders relax. "Why am I being offered my own biscuits?" he asks grumpily – and slumps back into his chair, muttering, "I know what they say about me, their vile calumnies: that I still cane boys; that I enjoy caning boys too much to surrender the privilege; that I enjoy the pain and degradation of young boys in, shall we say, some kind of immoral or Wildean fashion."

The boy shuffles to the edge of his chair. His face feels hot and he wants to leave. Mr Chandler slowly turns his head towards him. He *really* wants to leave now. "I'd better . . ." he starts. He doesn't get to the end of his sentence, though, before Mr Chandler interrupts. In this room, indeed, in this school in general, the boy hardly ever seems to reach the end of sentences.

Mr Chandler's tone has changed again – he seems to combine so many different voices, so many different moods – and now he sounds like he's giving a rehearsed speech, or defending himself in an imaginary courtroom. "While I readily confess my nostalgia for the good old days of canes, grammars and Latin; while I confess I believe wholeheartedly in the use of corporal punishment, and can see no future for educational discipline without it; while I view its renunciation as a symptom of the same left-wing lunacy which advocates unilateral disarmament on a national scale, and while I would also confess that I feel too old, too set in my ways to adjust to the new dispensation; despite all this, I can assert that my conscience is clear, and I have never once laid hands on a boy without good reason. I may be as full of sin as the next man; I may not be what in common parlance is known as a 'pleasant person,' whatever that is; but the very thought of gaining sadistic pleasure from the act of disciplining another human being is utterly repugnant to me. I would rather beat myself than have to administer punishment to others. It only causes me distress that such a thing is necessary. But unfortunately sometimes it *is* necessary – I truly believe it to be so. As a final resort, it is our stay against confusion, our last line of defence against educational anarchy."

Having reached the peroration of his speech, Mr Chandler pops the Custard Cream he's been holding into his mouth and sinks back into the armchair. He mutters while chewing, "That 'right-on' daughter of the '6os, Mrs Yaël, with her flower-print dresses and hippy songs, often takes great pleasure in telling me I am wrong, out-of-date, a dinosaur. 'Mr Chandler,' she says to me, 'you need to put that cane away. Those days are gone. Violence begets violence, don't you know.' Clearly, boy, I do not, cannot agree, and happily tell her so: violence stops violence, I tell her. Look at the War.

"I am aware I am being rather, shall we say, unprofessional, at least in the conventional sense, in speaking of another, and rather dubious, member of staff in this way. Nonetheless, I am assured, boy, of your tact and confidence in these matters."

The boy nods. It's not as if he has anyone to talk to anyhow, and only comprehends half of what Mr Chandler says.

"Careless talk, you see, has been the ruin of me," continues Mr Chandler, "the ruin, I tell you. I cannot abide it. Of course, I know what Mrs Yaël and her like whisper about me behind my back. And I also know from whence the rumours about my alleged sadistic predilections originate."

"From Mrs Yaël?" asks the boy, who's relaxed a little and is biting the crust off one of his sandwiches.

"No, boy. Even a hippy would not be so malicious as that. No, indeed, rumours in teaching are an omnipresent curse; but in my case the curse gained a certain momentum two or so years ago."

"How?" asks the boy, his cheeks full.

"It was during that damned strike, boy. Unfortunately, I happened to make clear my opinions on the industrial action to some of the pupils, through a few minor hints I dropped during one particular lesson. I would admit, with hindsight, that these hints may have been slightly ill-judged. I may have underestimated the passions of those involved. Still, by no means did I deserve the violent reaction I received in response, from both parents and pupils alike. After all, it should hardly have come as a surprise that I, a man of education and culture, from a different social class to most of those whom I teach, should be opposed, on principle, to their misguided cause. I was hardly going to align myself with Communists, Scargills and the appalling violence of so-called 'flying pickets,' was I?"

"So what happened?" asks the boy.

"I'm glad you ask. You are probably the only person who has asked for my side of the story thus far. Even my wife will not listen, seems uninterested, these days." He pauses, waiting for a quotation to come to the surface that's been nagging at him:

Come, let's away to prison:
We two alone will sing like birds i' the cage:
When thou dost ask me blessing, I'll kneel down,
And ask of thee forgiveness: so we'll live,
And pray, and sing, and tell old tales, and laugh
At gilded butterflies . . .

Afterwards, he smiles, murmuring "Beautiful, beautiful" under his breath, nibbling the edge of another Custard Cream – his only lunch. He seems to have forgotten everything else, apart from Custard Creams and *King Lear*.

The boy reminds him of the original question, which prompted the quotation, "So what happened?"

"Oh, I don't know really," says Mr Chandler. "Some of the parents complained, I believe, about my comments. The Head – who, between ourselves, is a lily-livered knave – compelled me to retract the statement in a letter to the parents concerned. It should have ended there – that was humiliating enough – but the parents were not satisfied, had expected the Head to terminate my employment. I suppose passions were, as they say on the News, running high. Because I was not dismissed, my suspicion is that pupils and a few irresponsible parents fanned the flames, as it were, of calumny – as a means of undermining my position in a more circuitous fashion."

"What does that mean?" asks the boy.

"Rumours. Ghastly rumours, dear boy, they spread them, and are still doing so. They continue to despise me even now. And I will tell you something else, boy: I can't help feeling that the school governors and Local Education Authority, who are all in each others' pockets, and who are all signed-up members of Her Majesty's Opposition, are – directly or indirectly – party to this vile conspiracy of whispers.

"'Foul whisperings are abroad,' boy," Mr Chandler mutters, distracted for a minute. He looks away from the TV, the Custard Creams, above the head of the new boy, to his right – where the window commands a view of a whole landscape, laid open like a wound – across the football field, over the fences, over the roofs of the housing estate, to the horizon, on which is silhouetted a derelict pithead.

"You know," says Mr Chandler, "they assail me, yet sometimes I want to tell them that, despite our (very great, of course) social, ideological and intellectual differences, the miners and I have much in common. We are both leftovers, as it were. We are both obsolete. We have both been consigned to the rubbish bin of history."

"I don't think that's true, sir. On the News it said . . ."

"The News, like the Law, boy, is an ass. In the words of our greatest Poet Laureate: 'a thousand types are gone / I care for nothing, all shall go.' We are all consigned to history's dustbin eventually." Mr Chandler sighs. "Sometimes I think perhaps I was wrong about the strike, about everything. Who knows. Perhaps, in retrospect, history will judge *them* better than myself."

He turns back to the TV, picks up another Custard Cream, and waves it at the boy. "And it's not all bad, is it, boy? At least it's a comfortable form of obsolescence in here. At least there are Custard Creams, cricket and my trusty cane nearby. At least I can sit in peace and quiet, and not have to listen to Mrs Yaël spouting 'aspirations' and 'mutual respect' in the staff room. Thankfully, you don't say a great deal, boy, which is a quality in yourself and a blessing to others. You should keep it that way."

6.

They're waiting for him on the way home from school. There are three of them – three girls, this time: Kez and two of her friends. They surround him in the alleyway, which leads down to the main road.

"If you say anything, or make a noise," says Kez, "it'll be worse." She's holding him by the wrist. She twists it, and pushes him down to the ground, as hard as Terry pushed her the previous day. He lands on his side, and stares up at the three girls, eyes wide. They lean over him. All three of them have sticks.

"Cos of you Terry won't talk to me," Kez snarls. "It's

your fucking fault, scab. Queer. You ruined it." She grinds her teeth to stop herself crying in front of the others.

He's crawling away — but knows it's futile.

"You won't get away this time," says Kez. "There's no library to hide in round here. No Chandler to run to. You're on your own, *faggot*." She spits on him. One of the other girls kicks him in the stomach for good measure.

"Please . . ." he murmurs.

The girl kicks him again. "Shut your gob and listen to Kezza."

"Don't you worry your little head," says Kez, "we're not *really* going to hurt you." All three of them are standing up straight now, flexing their sticks — which are canes they've taken from someone's garden — testing them on their palms, like Mr Chandler.

"I'll cane you, boy," sniggers one of the girls, in a deep, posh voice.

Kez glares at her, then says to them both, "Take down his trousers."

The boy tries to crawl away again. He's crying as they pull him back and rip his school trousers down.

"Yuck," one of the girls says, "yellow Y-fronts."

"Please," the new boy whimpers.

"Don't worry," says Kez, "like I said, this won't hurt. You obviously enjoy it. You must do, spending all your time with pervy Chandler."

She steps back. "Hold him down," she commands the other two girls. "It's my turn first."

She flexes the cane, judges the distance, the best angle. She thinks of how Terry has hurt her, how her father hurts her, how everyone seems to hurt everyone else.

Afterwards – after they've all finished with him, and Kez has had a second, third go – she steps on his fingers. "If you tell anyone about this," she says, "it'll be worse next time. And we'll tell everyone about what you and Chandler do in the library. Everyone."

She takes her foot off his fingers, and he scrambles to his feet, whimpering, dazed, holding his trousers up. She glances from him to the cane in her hand. Then she throws the cane away from her, down the alleyway, and rubs her hands on her skirt. She doesn't say anything to the two friends – merely turns her back on them, on him, and strides away, disgusted by everything.

7.

That evening, the boy sits on his grandpa's sofa, pretending to watch TV, pretending to be doing his homework, pretending he isn't hurting.

"Stop that bloody wriggling," his grandpa grunts every time he wakes up – sounding rather like someone else. The boy doesn't tell him why he can't sit still, and no-one can see the cuts and weals under his trousers. Now and then, the pain echoes through them and he grimaces, tears rising to his eyes. He doesn't yelp, though, doesn't say anything in response to his grandpa; he just waits for the snores to return.

From the corner behind the boy, to his right, he can hear his mum knitting, crying quietly about Dad. She thinks he doesn't know.

Open on his lap is his English homework. He can't concentrate on it. Instead, he keeps thinking of a letter he's been trying to write for some months now. He's drafted it dozens of times, but never reaches the end before he screws it up. It never sounds quite right; he never knows how to put it, or what exactly needs saying.

He sighs, gets up from the sofa. His grandpa mutters without opening his eyes, "Stop that bloody squirming, or I'll . . ." The boy hovers for a moment. His grandpa's threat ends with snores.

The boy tiptoes out of the room and comes back a minute later holding a notepad. His mother looks up. "For an English project," he whispers to her, waving the pad. "I have to write a letter." She nods and returns to knitting, sniffling.

He sits down and opens the pad. He writes his address in the right-hand corner, as the teacher showed him in his previous school – though now, of course, it's a different address, almost a different life.

Dear Jim, he writes, *a year ago my dad died and . . .* – and then he stops, sucking the end of the pen.

The letter is addressed to a white-haired guy on the TV who looks a bit like his grandpa, but with more smiles, fewer snores – a guy who grants wishes to kids. The wishes on the programme, though, are all things you can see or do, like riding on an elephant, or meeting Daley Thompson. How can the boy write what he wants, how can he put it into words: a safe place to go, a place where his mother isn't sad, and where no-one tries to hurt him. Places like that exist only on the telly, he thinks, only in the enclosed, bleached world of a BBC studio.

8.

Next lunchtime, the new boy walks awkwardly – still sore – to the library. There's no shout of "I'll cane you, boy" as he approaches, because the door is closed.

The boy hovers, shifting his weight from one leg to the other, wondering what to do. There's no-one else around, the corridor is quiet, except for muffled sounds from behind the door. He puts his ear against the wood.

He remembers the last time he did this, in a house a long way away, in a different life. Back then, he'd overheard crying and two voices, one high-pitched, one growlingly low, from within: "How on earth can I tell him?" "You've got to. He needs to know. He needs to be a man." "He's eleven, Dad." "That's old enough. His father's dead. You can't molly-coddle him any longer. There's been too much of that."

The boy shakes his head, as if to shake the memory out, and puts his head back against the library door. This time, what he hears through wood is indistinct, ambiguous. He thinks there is a voice, someone who may or may not be Mr Chandler mumbling, grunting; and there's also a noise – a swishing noise, and a thwack, as of something hard hitting something softer. The boy's body remembers that sound for him, and he almost falls over with sudden pain.

He backs away from the door, staring at it. Then he turns and runs down the corridor and out into the playground.

He spends the rest of lunch break standing alone in a corner of the playground, his sandwiches untouched. No-one speaks to him; no-one lays a finger on him. Terry and his mates aren't interested, and Kez almost winces when she sees him, as if she's been caned too. She walks quickly past, trying to laugh at something one of her friends is saying.

9.

The following day, the new boy passes the library door on the way to the playground. It's half-open, and a voice booms from within, "I'll cane you, boy."

Then Mr Chandler is suddenly there next to him, in the doorway, "Ah, is it you, boy?"

"Yes, sir. I think so."

"I thought it was." He pauses, rocking backwards and forwards on his heels. "Well, boy," he says, umming and ahhing, "are you watching the last day of the test match?"

"I suppose so, sir," says the boy, and he follows Mr Chandler into the library. Mr Chandler pushes the door shut behind them. The boy hesitates, stops halfway towards the chair.

"What's wrong, boy? Why are you standing there, gawping? The over is about to start."

The backs of the boy's legs are throbbing.

"I think I might go outside instead, sir."

Mr Chandler frowns. "Why? Don't you want to watch the cricket with . . . with your sandwiches?"

"No, sir, it's just . . ."

"Spit it out, boy. What's wrong with you?"

Not knowing how else to respond, the boy spits it out, "It's just that I heard something yesterday, sir."

"Heard what? What did you hear?" demands Mr

Chandler. "I told you, it's all lies, defaming an upstand-
ing member of an honourable profession in his declining
years. 'One doth not know / How much an ill word may
empoison liking.'"

"No, sir, I don't mean I heard one of the rumours. I
already know about them. I mean, I heard something
coming from in here."

"I fail to understand you, boy."

"I was listening at the door. I know that's the wrong
thing to do, sir, but the door was closed and I didn't know
if you were in or not or if I should disturb you. So I was
listening and I heard . . . noises through the door."

"What kinds of noises?"

Again, the boy's legs throb. "Cane noises," he says. "I'm
sorry, sir, I didn't mean to eavesdrop. But I don't want to
be caned, and you're not supposed to do it anymore, and I
thought you didn't, and you said you didn't, and . . ." The
boy runs out of "ands" and breath at the same moment.

Mr Chandler nods slowly, and mutters, "I see." He turns
away, and steps over to his armchair. He lowers himself
into it. "I see. You heard these 'cane noises,' as you put it,
and assumed that I was administering, illegally, corporal
punishment to some other boy."

"Or girl," says the boy, "I thought it might be K . . ."

"Girl?" asks Mr Chandler. "*Girl?* I have never in my life
laid hands on a girl. What do you take me for?"

"I don't know," says the boy, honestly.

"I'm not a monster," says Mr Chandler. "God forbid I,
a gentleman who once taught in a grammar school system
which was the envy of the world, would lay hands on a
girl."

"But, sir," says the boy, feeling that they are – as usual – drifting away from the subject at hand, "you're not supposed to 'lay hands' on a boy either nowadays."

"Indeed," says Mr Chandler. He hesitates, purses his lips, seems to be mulling something over. Then he nods, as if he's come to a decision. "Boy," he says. "I want you to see something."

The boy is tempted to turn and run.

"Boy, come closer."

The boy doesn't move.

"Boy, come here, or I really *will* cane you."

The boy takes a couple of steps towards Mr Chandler.

Mr Chandler has taken off his jacket and is rolling up the right sleeve. The boy is ready to run.

"Look," says Mr Chandler. The boy doesn't know what he's meant to be looking at. "Look, for God's sake," says Mr Chandler, pointing at his own right arm.

The arm is very hairy; clearly visible through the hairs, though, are half a dozen white and red welts, like the ones on the boy's legs and bottom.

"It's surprisingly difficult to cane oneself," says Mr Chandler, in a matter-of-fact voice, "but practice over some years makes perfect, as they say." He looks up at the boy and shrugs his shoulders. "And, as far as I am aware, it is not yet illegal."

He rolls his sleeve back and puts his jacket on. The boy doesn't know what to say, doesn't really understand, so just steps over to his usual chair, and sits next to Mr Chandler. He considers asking, "Why, sir? Why would you do something horrible like that to yourself?" but the question remains unspoken. From his own eleven years of experience, he knows that the question "Why?" is sometimes a dead-end.

Instead of asking dead-end questions, they both sit for a while, in silence, watching the cricket. Now and then, Mr Chandler makes an approving or disapproving noise in response to what's going on. As the boy noticed on his first visit, Mr Chandler's head moves slightly with the ball, as if by instinct.

Between overs, Mr Chandler mumbles: "Of course, you can now go away and laugh with your friends at poor Mr Chandler, who threatens everyone and instead hurts only himself."

"Oh no, sir, I won't do that. I haven't got any . . ."

"Soon, no doubt, everyone will know. But what does it signify to me? It is a mere bauble in comparison with other crimes of which I am regularly accused."

"Honestly, sir, I won't tell anyone."

Mr Chandler raises his hands, palms upwards, as if beseeching someone or something. "How can I believe you, boy, when I have believed so many, who have gone on to desert me? 'My friends forsake me like a memory lost.'"

The boy is quiet for a few seconds. Then he bends over and rolls up one of his trouser legs, above the knee. "See, sir. I've got the same marks."

Mr Chandler looks down, and frowns. "It is my turn not to comprehend now, boy."

"I've got the same marks as you, sir. And like you, sir, it's a secret. The marks, they go all the way up my legs and on . . . and on my bottom, sir."

"Why?" asks Mr Chandler. "Have you been hurting yourself too, boy?"

"No," says the boy. "Some girls did it to me."

"The girls who were chasing you the other day?"

The boy doesn't say anything in response. He rolls his trouser leg back down to his ankle.

"Why did they do this to you, boy?" asks Mr Chandler.

The boy doesn't mention Mr Chandler's part in the girls' motivation: "Because they said I was from Scabland."

"Scabland*s*?"

"Yes, sir. Something like that."

Mr Chandler frowns. "But that's ridiculous, boy. You're English. You can't be from Scablands. As far as I understand it, the Scablands are located in the godforsaken nation known as the United States of America. I can appreciate, maybe even share, your tormentors' anti-American feeling, but they've clearly taken it out on the wrong victim."

"But, sir, I don't think they mean . . ."

"In fact, we can look it up. What is this library for – other than watching test matches, of course – than the deepening of our knowledge of the world?"

Mr Chandler gets up from his chair, and strides over to one of the shelves in front of him. He slides out a large book, *Encyclopaedia of World Geology and Geography*. Flicking through it, he mutters to himself: "Q . . . not much there . . . R . . . S . . . S . . . Salt Mining . . . Saskatoon . . . Saudi Arabia . . ."

"But, sir, I don't think they mean Scabland in Amer . . ."

Mr Chandler isn't listening – perhaps deliberately ignoring any suggestion that "Scabland" might refer to something closer to home.

"Ah, here we are. Yes, I was right: *Scablands, also known as Channeled Scablands, a barren plateau of approximately*

2,000 square miles in Washington State, USA, marked by deep fissures. Some of these fissures, which are called coulees, are hundreds of feet deep and many miles in length. Geologists believe the coulees may have been formed by cataclysmic floods during the last ice age." Mr Chandler glances up from the book. "Your leg looked a bit like a mini-Scablands, boy."

The boy nods. Mr Chandler shuts the book and slides it back onto the shelf. He sits down.

"Would you like me to bring this . . . incident to the attention of the lily-livered headmaster, so he can half-heartedly reprimand the culprits?"

"No, sir."

"Would you like me to reprimand them instead – wholeheartedly with my cane? I would undertake such a commission with relish, whatever the consequences to my retirement package."

"No thank you, sir. And please don't tell my mum. I'd prefer no-one but you and me know about it." The boy thinks for a moment. "If you don't tell anyone about my legs, sir, I won't tell anyone about your arms."

"Agreed," says Mr Chandler, proffering his index finger for the boy to shake. "And thank *you*, boy."

"Why thank me?"

"Because your discretion in the small matter of my own, shall we say, injuries is greatly appreciated. Until today, only my wife has seen the state of my arms, although, with characteristic tact, she never mentions it. For the most part, they are covered in shirt or pyjama sleeves, anyway. These days, my skin is rarely exposed to hers and vice versa. 'Even the dearest that I loved the best / Are strange – nay, rather stranger, than the rest.'" He squints for a moment at the

TV, as if he's staring at something very small, very far away – and when he speaks again, his speech seems similarly aimed at some distant point, something out of reach. "In that sphere, you see, I find it almost impossible to perform these days."

"But sir, you're very good at performing," says the boy, confused. "You talk Shakespeare and poetry and stuff like no-one I've ever heard."

Mr Chandler comes back to earth, and half laughs, half coughs, "Well, well, that's very good of you to say. Maybe I would have been better suited to the acting life, after all. 'A high silk hat and a silver cane,' *et cetera et cetera.*"

He pats the boy's hand, which is resting on the arm of the chair. Then he glances down at their hands. "I suppose I'm not meant to do *that* either," says Mr Chandler. "Everything's so confusing nowadays, boy. I can't seem to get a handle on it. Mrs Yaël *et al* tell us we shouldn't administer corporal punishment, and spout claptrap about love and respect for children. Yet at the same time if we – and by we, I mean people such as myself – express the slightest so-called affection, we are immediately under suspicion for other outrages, perpetrated on the innocent. Sometimes, I feel I am in a bubble, unable to touch anything or anyone. Or rather, to mix my metaphors, I am between a rock and hard place, frying pan and fire, Scylla and Charybdis, in everything I do." Mr Chandler shakes his head, and mumbles like an echo, "Scylla and Charybdis, Scylla and Charybdis," over and again, quieter and quieter – until his lips are moving, but no sound is coming out.

On the television, someone bowls, and the batsman

swings. The ball connects with the bat and is lofted high, high above the cricketers. The camera follows the ball's flight – as it arcs for six over fielders and spectators. Mr Chandler's eyes, then head, follow it too. The ball sails over the crowds – as though heading out of the stadium, heavenwards – and finally disappears from shot, lost to the camera. But Mr Chandler's head carries on following its imagined trajectory – and now he's leaning over the side of the armchair – and now he's bent over, almost perpendicular with the arm – and now he's sitting on the arm, his whole body stretched out in a diagonal line, as if he's reaching out, to catch the ball – and now he's sliding, falling onto the floor, his feet still on the arm of the chair, his left arm outstretched – and now –

"Mr Chandler?" The boy laughs then frowns. "Mr Chandler? The ball's gone, Mr Chandler."

The boy gets off his chair, and crouches down by Mr Chandler's face. The side pressed against the floor looks stretched.

"Mr Chandler? Why are you on the floor, sir?"

"Please," comes a croak from the stretched face. "Please. Find. Another. Teacher."

The boy hesitates. "Are you all right, sir?"

"Please, boy. Another teacher." He grinds his teeth: "No ambulance."

The boy gets to his feet and runs. He runs out of the room and down the corridor. He runs past the prefect, who tries to grab him. "You're going the wrong way down . . ."

"Oh shut up," says the boy.

He runs round the corner, down another corridor.

He runs past an art room, which is empty.

He pushes past a group of girls. One of them is Kez. "Get out of the way," he shouts. Kez flattens herself against the wall to let him through.

He reaches a music room, and skids to a halt, because he can hear piano playing, and a teacher's voice inside.

He doesn't bother to knock.

"Mrs Yaël!" he shouts.

The music is broken off. A pupil peers round the side of the piano. Mrs Yaël strides up to the new boy. "What is the meaning of . . ."

"Please, Mrs Yaël," says the boy, panting, bent double, "please come. It's Mr Chandler. In the library."

Mrs Yaël nods at the piano player, "Continue with the Lennon," – and then allows herself to be led by the new boy back to the library.

They find Mr Chandler still on the floor, next to his armchair.

"What on earth are you doing down there, man?" asks Mrs Yaël.

He looks up at Mrs Yaël from the floor, and slurs, "Oh, God. It's you."

She kneels down in front of him, saying to the new boy, "Go quickly and tell the office we need an ambulance."

Mr Chandler's hand shoots out and grabs the boy's leg before he can move. "No ambulance," he hisses. "They call my wife. But no ambulance."

"You need a doctor, Mr Chandler," says Mrs Yaël.

"No," hisses Mr Chandler, with some difficulty. "Haven't seen a doctor in twenty years. Not going to start now."

Mrs Yaël tuts. "Such an exasperating man."

The half of Mr Chandler's face which isn't flattened against the floor tries to grin. "I know." He groans. "First, help me up. Please."

The boy and Mrs Yaël aren't sure how to do this. They pull him by the arms along the floor, so his legs are no longer propped up against the chair. Then they roll him onto his front and hold him under his arms. There's a lot of grunting, puffing and panting from all three of them; but eventually, Mrs Yaël and the new boy put Mr Chandler's arms round their shoulders, and manage to pull him to his feet. The boy is bent double, shaking, almost crying – crushed downwards into the floor. Adults, adulthood, growing up, growing old: these things seem very heavy, he thinks.

Mrs Yaël kicks Mr Chandler's armchair round with one foot, so it's behind him, and they drop him into it.

"I don't care what he says," Mrs Yaël gasps between breaths. "Go and call an ambulance."

As he's leaving the room, the new boy glances round to see Mr Chandler slumped in the armchair. His lips are moving automatically, muttering something Shakespearean to himself.

Then the boy turns away to leave the room. He doesn't know that this will be the last time he will ever see Mr Chandler: that the bell will soon go, and he'll be sent straight back to lessons after asking the office to call an ambulance; and that the ambulance will take Mr Chandler away from school for good, to permanent retirement and a different kind of limbo.

No-one will tell the new boy, of course, what has happened. No-one will give him a second thought. For years afterwards, on passing the library door, the boy-who-is-no-longer-new will expect to hear, "I'll cane you, boy," as if the threat might linger as an echo, a ghost, a school's repressed past. But he never does, and the threat has gone.

Acknowledgements

Thanks for their help, expert advice, support and encouragement to Amanda Angus, Karen Argent, Francis Bowdery, Will Buckingham, Rowland Cotterill, Nick Everett, Cathy Galvin, Andrew Lees, Jamie McGarry, Jane Roberts, John Schad, Farhana Shaikh, Hannah Stevens, Karen Stevens, Ashley Stokes, Jose Varghese, Robin Webber-Jones, Harry Whitehead.

Thanks to the brilliant Jen and Chris Hamilton-Emery, and everyone at Salt Publishing.

Thanks and love, as always, to my mother, Robin, Anna, Karen, Helen, Ben, Sam, Naomi, Erin, Finola, Tancred, Conal, Dylan, Ivy, Hazel, and, of course, Miranda, Rosalind and Maria.

Earlier versions of these stories appeared in the following publications. Many thanks to the editors and publishers involved.

'Adagietto' was first published by Coral Press, 2019.
'A Sentimental Story' was first published in *Fictive Dream*, 2017.
'Bee in the Bonnet' was first published in *Axon: Creative Explorations*, 2022.

Acknowledgements

'Bubble Man' was first published by *Fictive Dream*, 2020.

'But what happens after?' was first published in *The End: Fifteen Endings to Fifteen Paintings*, Unthank Books, 2016.

'Changelessness' was first published in *Bystander Anthology*, Laundrette Books, 2017.

'Heat Death' was first published in *Eunoia Review*, 2019.

'He never writes to me no more' was first published in *Speaking Words: Writing for Read Aloud*, and *Crystal Voices*, Crystal Clear Creators, 2005 and 2015.

'J. S. Bach, Double Violin Concerto for Two Violins' was first published in *Unthology 9*, 2017.

'Not a horror story' was first published in *Sleep is a Beautiful Colour: National Flash-Fiction Day 2017 Anthology*, Gumbo Press, 2017.

'Outside the Circle' was first published in *The Cabinet of Heed*, 2019.

'Scablands' was first published by Fairlight Books, 2018.

'Staring Girl' was first published in *Lucifer Magazine*, 2017.

'Tell me what you know' was first published in *Burning House Press*, 2017.

'Till Life' was first published in *Strands Lit Sphere*, 2020.

'Trial' was first published by *Lunate Fiction*, 2020.

'You Keep It' was first published by the *Letter Press Project*, 2019.

'Zoë K.' was first published in *Lost and Found: Stories of Home by Leicestershire Writers*, Dahlia Publishing, 2016.

This book has been typeset by
SALT PUBLISHING LIMITED
using Granjon, a font designed by George W. Jones
for the British branch of the Linotype company in the
United Kingdom. It is manufactured using Holmen
Bulky News 52gsm, a Forest Stewardship Council™
certified paper from the Hallsta Paper Mill in Sweden.
It was printed and bound by Clays Limited in Bungay,
Suffolk, Great Britain.

CROMER
GREAT BRITAIN
MMXXIII